# The Bone Collector's Son

# The Bone Collector's Son

## by Paul Yee

VANCOUVER   LONDON

*For my father,*
*Gordon Ngoon-ling (1910-1957),*
*whose bones rest in Saskatchewan.*
*- P.Y.*

Hardback edition published in 2003 in Canada and Great Britain
and paperback edition published in 2004 in Canada and Great Britain by
Tradewind Books • www.tradewindbooks.com

Distribution and representation in Canada by
Hushion House • orders@gtwcanada.com

Distribution and representation in the UK by
Turnaround • www.turnaround-uk.com

J/Middle School

Text copyright © 2003 by Paul Yee
Cover art © 2003 by Shaoli Wang
Book & cover design by Jacqueline Wang

Printed in Canada on recycled paper.
6 8 10 9 7 5

Cataloguing-in-Publication Data for this book is available from The British Library.

National Library of Canada Cataloguing in Publication

Yee, Paul
     The bone collector's son / Paul Yee.

ISBN 1-896580-25-4 (bound).-ISBN 1-896580-50-5 (pbk.)

     1. Chinatown (Vancouver, B.C.)--Juvenile fiction. 2. Chinese--
Canada--Juvenile fiction. 3. Ghost stories, Canadian (English) I. Title.

PS8597.E3B66 2003          jC813'.54          C2002-911515-9

The author gratefully acknowledges the financial assistance of the Canada Council for the Arts during the writing of this book.

Map (overleaf)
*Panoramic view of the city of Vancouver, British Columbia 1898,* by J. C. McLagan; Toronto Lithographing Co. Limited. Vancouver, BC: Vancouver World Printing and Publishing Company, Limited, 1898.

Rare Books and Special Collections, University of British Columbia Library.

View this map in detail at www.tradewindbooks.com

*The publisher thanks the Wormers Book Club and Frances Woodward of the University of British Columbia Library for their help.*

*The publisher also thanks the Canada Council for the Arts and the British Columbia Arts Council for their support.*

Canada Council   Conseil des Arts
for the Arts      du Canada

BRITISH
COLUMBIA
ARTS COUNCIL

UPPER FALSE CREEK FLATS

BURRARD

1. CHINATOWN  2. CEMETERY.  3. CAMBIE BRIDGE.  4. FALSE CREEK.  5. FAIRVIEW.

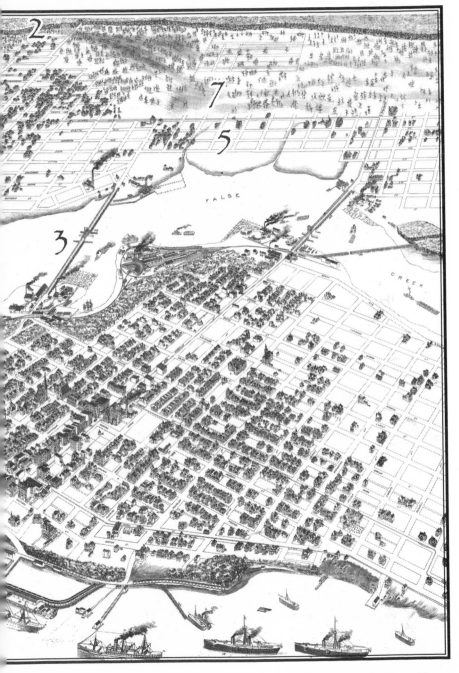

6. WESTMINSTER STREET, NOW MAIN STREET. 7. HOSPITAL. 8. CITY HALL.

# A Boy from Chinatown

# Chapter One

B ING FROZE AT THE SIGHT OF TWO DARK FIGURES FLOATING AMONG THE GRAVESTONES. NO ONE WAS SUPPOSED TO BE HERE, NOT THIS EARLY IN THE MORNING.

*Ghosts!* Bing thought, and before he could stop himself, he was mumbling as fast as he could:

> *The Lord is my shepherd;*
> *I shall not want.*
> *He maketh me to lie down in green pastures;*
> *He leadeth me beside the still waters.*
> *Though I walk through the valley of the shadow of death...*

"Stupid fool, you think a Jesus prayer will help you now?" his father, Ba, muttered in Chinese. "Hurry!" he growled, heading toward the ghostly figures as if they were harmless.

Bing had tossed and turned all night, thinking desperately of ways to keep away any cemetery ghosts. He had thought of stealing the protective charm, written in red on a square of paper and pinned above Uncle Sing's bed. He had thought of pretending to be sick. But Ba would have dragged him along anyway. Bing had even considered a phoney tumble down the stairs to fake a sprained ankle. But Ba would have called him a weakling. Finally, Bing had decided to recite *Psalm 23* at the cemetery if he saw any ghosts.

"I fear no evil," continued Bing in a whisper. He finished the psalm with a loud *Amen* and hoped God would hear him.

A thick forest surrounded the graveyard. Silence hung in the morning air. A hawk soared high above in a long, lazy circle.

As he walked gingerly toward the gravestones, Bing dragged a heavy pickaxe behind him. His father walked ahead, holding two shovels on his right shoulder with his right hand and a burlap bag in his left hand.

Bing kept his eyes fixed on the two figures at the grave, trying to assess the threat they posed. But he couldn't see their faces no matter how hard he squinted.

*Are they going to leap into the pit, their jackets flapping up like capes? Or will they fly into the forest, cawing like huge black crows?* Bing thought.

They seemed to hover in the mist that hung over the graveyard. As he drew closer, Bing realized they were grieving mourners. One was a woman, wearing a wide-brimmed hat and a long skirt. Her male companion wore a dark suit and cradled a hat in his arm.

Bing breathed a sigh of relief. *I'm too old to be scared by this. I'm almost fifteen,* he thought.

As father and son approached, the two black-clad mourners glanced up and turned their backs on Bing and his father, just like all the other white people who treated Chinese rudely.

Bing dragged his pickaxe across a headstone. The sharp sound caused the two mourners to spin around, and Bing smiled.

"Over here!" Ba shouted.

Bing continued to drag his pickaxe all the way across the white people's section of the cemetery. Most of the graves were crowned with elaborate granite and marble headstones. Some headstones rose like fence-posts, while others were flat on the ground, almost invisible in the grass. Wilted bouquets lay on many graves.

In the Chinese section, the graves were marked with wooden boards. Some were thick, solid planks with deeply carved Chinese words and names. Other markers were raw timber with crudely scratched names. Weather and time had darkened and split the wood.

Ba hobbled from row to row, reading the years and names, noting those graves that needed his attention. Bing noticed that the ground had sunk in front of some markers, as if the bones had already been removed. He swallowed hard and let the handle of his pickaxe fall to the ground.

"Hey, lift that!" Ba looked up and scowled. "Show some respect. And watch your feet. You're walking on people!"

"Dead people," Bing retorted. He was sick of Ba's shouting. "Look, the ground isn't level. Maybe the bones have already been collected."

"You fool," Ba snorted. "The soil has settled and the coffins have collapsed. Of course the ground sinks. Don't they teach you anything useful at school?"

*I wish I were somewhere far away,* Bing thought, making a sour face his father couldn't see. *If only Ba hadn't suddenly come back to town. If only Ba weren't weighed down by gambling debts. Then I could have gone fishing at the harbour today.*

Ba stopped by one grave and read the faded inscription on the wooden marker. Then he put down the shovels, reached inside the burlap bag and pulled out a large white cloth. He laid the cloth flat on the ground next to the grave. Then he grabbed the pickaxe from Bing and swung it over his shoulder and into the ground with a thud.

Bing jumped.

Never before had he seen his father release such strength. It was a wild kind of power, like Uncle Won's horses when they were spooked, whinnying and rearing up, front legs lashing the air. The pickaxe sank deeper each time it hit the ground. Sweat slid down Ba's face, and when he removed his jacket, wet patches of shirt clung to his skin.

Bing watched so intently that he was startled when someone snarled, "What the hell are you doing?"

A man with a bushy moustache and burnt red nose had come up behind Ba.

Ba plunged the axe into the ground again, and Moustache-man shoved him.

"What the hell are you doing?" Moustache-man repeated.

*If a white man wants to fight,* Bing recalled his father's advice, *you walk away. Walk away, even if you think you're stronger and can win.*

Moustache-man spat out a wad of tobacco. His tattered suspenders held up stiff, mud-spattered trousers. He shoved a fist into Ba's face.

"Get out, Chinaman, before I call the police."

*Go on, fight! Hit him!* Bing wanted to shout. *Hit him hard! Put your fist right through him! Kick high and jump over him in a flying leap!*

He recalled seeing a troupe of acrobats at a town festival back in China. Two men, stripped to the waist, flexed their muscles, which gleamed with oil. Then they somersaulted backward through the air. They attacked one another with fists and bare feet, spinning and twisting so fast that Bing couldn't tell if it was a real fight. He had wanted to stay and watch, but Grandmother yanked him away by the ear.

"This say I can take Shum's bones," Ba said in English, fishing a letter out of his pocket.

"You're digging up the bones?" Moustache-man squinted at the gold-embossed letterhead.

"Send Shum home to China," said Ba.

"How many graves have you already dug up?"

"In this province two hundred, maybe three hundred, maybe five hundred."

"Why? Our Canadian soil not good enough for you Chinamen?"

Bing hoped his father wouldn't explain further; that would only make Moustache-man angrier.

Ba was a bone collector. Several years after Chinese workers died, the bone collector would dig up their bones, clean them and ship them home to China for reburial near their ancestors.

In his village in China, Bing had followed Mother and Grandmother into the hills every spring. There they swept the family tombs and burned offerings and incense to honour their ancestors. Many Chinese men travelled far away to find work, but their final resting-place was always their own village and the land their families had known for generations.

Moustache-man's lips twitched. "Good riddance," he muttered and marched off.

"That bastard can't even read," sneered Ba, switching back to Chinese. "Get the shovel and start digging."

Bing stepped toward the foot of the grave.

"Not there, stupid fool! Here!" His father pointed to the middle of the plot. "You know how tall Shum was? No, you don't! So, if you start at the bottom, you might miss him altogether."

Bing inched closer to the middle of the grave as his father's foot jammed the shovel into the earth. But when Bing struck the shovel with his foot, the ground didn't yield. It was like rock.

"Use your body weight to press down," Ba said, handing Bing the shovel he himself had been using. "Use this one; its handle is shorter."

Bing managed to move a few handfuls of soil.

"Toss the dirt farther away," Ba said. "You want it falling back into the grave? You want to do twice the work?"

All morning long, Ba shouted orders: "Dig here! No, dig there! Use your legs! Don't stand there! You'll flatten the soil and make it harder to dig."

Bing learned how to raise the shovel high and then slam it into the ground before jumping onto its blade. The deeper he went, the more firmly the earth was packed. When he bent close to the ground, a dank smell made him gag. It was a too familiar scent. It was just like in China where the odours floated up from the river's edge, through rice fields, vegetable patches and pigpens.

Every night, Bing would watch as his mother sat in the courtyard picking her fingernails clean with a hairpin. Then she would scrub her feet, mud swirling into the clear water. After she finished, she would wash his feet too, tickling them to make him laugh.

Bing wished Mother and Grandmother were here now to soothe the pale blisters that had begun to erupt on his hands. When the pain increased, Ba tossed him strips of cloth to wind around the swelling, just the way boxers wrapped their fingers before matches.

As father and son dug deeper, the morning sun burned hotter.

*Too bad all the trees are at the edges of the cemetery,* Bing thought, yearning for shade, for a breeze, for any excuse to leave.

Bing and Ba took a break and drank from jars of water they had brought from home.

"How far down do we dig?" Bing asked impatiently.

"Not too deep," Ba said, fanning himself with his cap. "People want the bones to come clean quickly; so they bury the body close to the surface. There the skin falls off faster."

Bing and Ba lowered themselves into the pit when it became deep enough. The space was so small that they kept bumping into one another as they worked. Dirt seeped into Bing's boot as the ground compressed beneath his heel. Finally, his spade hit something solid and slid across a smooth surface.

*A skull!* Bing thought, scrambling out of the grave.

"Throw me the small trowel," called Ba. "You'll find it in the burlap bag."

He squatted and ran his fingers through the soil carefully. Bing backed away and his father laughed.

"It's only a big rock," Ba said, holding it up.

Bing sighed and slid back into the pit. It was late morning before they found the first body part.

"An arm!" Ba announced, brandishing a long bone with gnarled knobs at both ends. He peered at the dirt at his feet and frowned.

"That's strange," he continued, "usually there are splinters of wood before we reach the bones. This was probably a poor man who couldn't afford a coffin."

Bing climbed out of the grave and stared down at the bone. It was brownish and flecked with dark patches.

*Are those bloodstains?* he wondered.

"What are you afraid of? Ghosts?" Ba asked.

Then Ba thrust the bone at him and Bing backed away, unwinding the cloth strips around his blisters.

"Human bones are all like this," continued Ba, scornfully.

Then he climbed out of the grave and placed the bone on the white cloth he had laid out.

"You stupid fool! There are no such things as ghosts. If there were, I'd have starved to death a long time ago," he said.

*Then why do people tell ghost stories and burn offerings?* Bing thought. *Everyone in Chinatown believes in ghosts.*

Bing wanted to run away, but his legs wouldn't move. He felt stinging in the corners of his eyes and willed himself not to cry. If he lost control, Ba would call him stupid and useless.

Mopping his forehead with a grimy rag, Ba went back to work. He unearthed the rest of the bones—arm bones, shoulder blades, a ribcage and hand fragments—and lay them carefully onto the white cloth so as not to lose a single piece.

Bing watched in a daze, as though he were trapped in a strange dream. The sun beat down on him and scorched his back. He dared not move or turn his face away. It was bad enough to be flouting his father's orders. But if he walked off and didn't even watch, that would show a lack of respect and bring on a beating for sure. He stared at the growing pile of bones and imagined them suddenly flying up to form a skeleton that reached out to choke the life out of him. He shuddered and recalled an old Chinese ghost story he'd once heard.

*One night long ago in China, an opera troupe was invited to a mansion far out in the countryside. When the musicians and singers arrived, young men and women dressed in fine silks were laughing and playing games. The hostess introduced herself, welcomed the troupe and requested love scenes from romantic operas. She asked that they avoid scenes with powerful gods or heavenly fairies and promised to reward them handsomely in silver.*

The actors agreed and donned their costumes. At the end of each scene, the partygoers applauded and called for more. The singers saw much wine and fine food being served and expected a share too. But when they tried to take a break, the hostess cried out, "Please continue."

When they asked for refreshments, she replied, "In a while, in a while."

The singing proceeded, but soon the troupe members grew weary. They decided to irritate their hostess by playing a short scene with Guan Gung, the fiery God of War. One actor donned the red-painted mask and flowing beard of the god. But as soon as he appeared on stage, the mansion melted into thin air. The guests, the tempting food and wine and the lanterns all vanished.

The actors found themselves in a graveyard before a fresh tomb. Shivering in the sudden cold, they bent to read the inscription and learned their hostess was a young woman who had recently died. They realized her guests had been others who had suffered early deaths. If the mighty God of War had not appeared on stage, the actors would have been trapped forever in the realm of the ghosts.

"What's the matter with you?" Ba demanded, beginning to wipe the bones. "I told you before, there's nothing to fear."

He dampened rags with water from their drinking jars. "Take this."

Bing didn't move.

"I said, take this!" shouted Ba. "This is just a bone. It's no different from a tree branch! I tell you, there are things a hundred times more frightening in this world! Don't you want to grow up? You'd better start learning now!"

Ba pried open Bing's fist and shoved in the wet cloth. Bing resisted with all his might, but his father was stronger. The smell of Ba's sweat and tobacco was overwhelming. Suddenly, tears exploded from Bing's eyes, and he ran to the cemetery fence and threw up in great heaving gasps.

Shamed and shaking, Bing crouched in the shade. When he finally returned to the pit, his father was combing the soil with his fingers.

"So strange," Ba muttered. "There's no skull."

Bing felt relieved. *The skull's eye sockets would have kept me up all night,* he thought.

"Damned waste!" Ba said. He placed the bones, carefully bundled in white cloth, into the burlap sack. "The Council won't send Shum's bones home without his head. All this work, and now we won't get a single penny."

Bing turned away in disgust. His father was such a failure. He had one of the worst jobs in Chinatown, and he still couldn't do it right.

"Why don't you change jobs?" Bing asked.

"Why?" Ba demanded. "What's the matter?"

"Other kids say you're dirty." Bing looked away. "They won't come near me."

"Of course I'm dirty! I dig in the ground."

"They're not talking about the mud."

"They're scared," Ba snorted. "That's all. And their mothers don't know how to raise them. They have stones for brains. Don't pay them any mind!"

That was easy for Ba to say. He didn't have to go to school and watch the boys play stickball without including him.

# Chapter Two

BY THE TIME THE STREETCAR SCREECHED TO A HALT NEAR THE CEMETERY, THE SUN HAD DROPPED BELOW THE TREETOPS. TWO LINES OF STEEL RAILS RAN ALONG THE CENTRE OF A ROAD THAT CUT THROUGH THE DENSE FOREST. THE LINE STRETCHED NORTH ALL THE WAY TO DOWNTOWN VANCOUVER AND SOUTH TO THE RIVER AT NEW WESTMINSTER.

Bing scrambled to his feet, the heavy pickaxe in his hand and the shovels tied with sturdy ropes to his back. He felt glad to be finally heading back to Chinatown.

After Ba hoisted the bulging sack of bones onto the streetcar, Bing followed, shovels clanking. They took seats at the back. Bing leaned the pickaxe against the bench and slid to the window as the ticket collector approached them.

*Would the driver have let us aboard if he knew what was inside Ba's sack?* Bing wondered. *What do people think he's carrying? Corn cobs?*

He wanted to jump up, point at Ba and shout, *'Look, that man, he's carrying human bones in a bag!'*

Women would faint and children would scream, while men scrambled helter-skelter for the door. The conductor would throw Ba and his bones off the streetcar, and he would have to walk all the way back to Chinatown.

That thought brought a broad smile to Bing's face.

The streetcar lurched forward. The engine hum surged loudly and then died with a sudden click. The car stopped dead in its tracks.

Bing stood up, but all he could see were women's hats decorated with flowers and feathers, turning from side to side. He poked his head out the window.

*Has the trolley pole slipped off the cable?* he wondered.

He had leaned halfway out the window before he could see that the trolley pole was still properly connected to the electric wire above.

"Stupid fool, get your head back in here!" Ba growled.

"The broom's all right!" the ticket collector shouted to the driver, who fiddled nervously at his gears and pedals.

"Fetch me a good horse," grumbled a passenger, fanning himself with a boater hat. "A man never wastes his time riding a horse."

"They'll need a team of oxen to pull this car to the station," said another, checking a pocket watch chained to his vest.

All the passengers were annoyed and their voices rose with impatience.

*The next car will arrive,* Bing thought, *and it won't be able to go any further until our streetcar is moved. We'll have to sit here sweating, with a canvas sack full of human bones next to our seats.*

"What's the matter with this streetcar?" Ba swore in Chinese. "Can't they get it to run?"

Bing watched the ticket collector tug at the cable connected to the trolley pole. He broke the connection between the pole and the wire and then gingerly swung the bobbing pole back into place. It took several tries to get proper alignment; but when the motor didn't stir, he banged his fist on the side of the car.

"Ladies and gentlemen!" called the driver. "I'm sorry, but I'm afraid I have to ask you all to get off."

That sparked a commotion.

"This is outrageous!" someone shouted.

"Is the company sending carriages?" demanded another person.

"I demand you refund my fare!" said a third.

"Can't you fellows fix this?" asked someone else at the same time.

"We have to get off," Bing said loudly in English to Ba, as he seized the pickaxe and stumbled out the door.

*I'll show them I don't have to ask other Chinese to translate for me everywhere I go,* Bing thought.

Ba followed with the bag of bones on his back, swearing furiously. "Who wants to sit in this old broken thing?"

As soon as Ba's feet hit the ground, Bing heard a loud crackle, followed by a steady hum. He looked up at the streetcar. The power had returned, and the car pitched forward as its wheels bit into the rails.

"Hey!" shouted Ba. "Wait for us!"

But the car sped away, rumbling smoothly over the track. Bing and his father were left behind.

Bing dropped the pickaxe in a shady spot under the trees. He was hot and tired and thirsty. No water was left in their jars. The shovels on his back were getting heavier. A mosquito circled his ear, and Bing flicked his fingers at it.

*Going anywhere with Ba always turns into a disaster,* Bing thought.

Ba stomped over and set down the sack of bones.

"Those bastards! They just don't want Chinese riding in their car. Good thing we hadn't paid our fare yet!"

"There was no electricity," Bing pointed out.

"No power? How did the car get going?" Ba lifted one hand to cuff him.

Bing pulled back to a safe distance.

"The electricity starts and stops all the time. Even at school, the lights go out every now and then. That's the way it is."

"You think you're so smart, don't you?" sneered his father. But he lowered his fist.

Bing looked away. *No use even talking to Ba,* he thought.

When the next streetcar rolled toward them, they clambered on. Again they found seats at the back. But just as the driver released the brake, the power died abruptly again. A grim silence settled over the car, and Bing felt a chill creep up his spine. He glanced over at Ba.

*Doesn't he find this coincidence a bit strange?* Bing wondered.

But Ba was simply leaning back with his arms crossed over his chest and his legs sticking straight out.

The passengers muttered fitfully to one another as the ticket collector jumped off to adjust the trolley pole.

Bing watched him strain at the taut rope and thought, *Maybe the cable is worn at this spot. Maybe the electrical current isn't running properly here and that's why both streetcars have stalled. Or maybe it has something to do with the bones.*

A motorcar honked its horn and roared past them, leaving behind a cloud of dust. The people on the streetcar covered their mouths and noses.

"Please be patient," the driver said. "We'll have this figured out in a minute."

Bing jumped to his feet and tugged at Ba.

"The conductor said to get off," Bing said. He had a plan.

"He did?" Ba asked.

Bing dragged the pickaxe off the streetcar, stood well away and watched for Ba to come down the stairs. He waited to see if his theory about the bones was right. The very instant that his father's feet touched the ground, Bing heard a click as the electric current came alive and the streetcar sped away.

"Don't those stinking bastards want my money?" demanded Ba. He set down the sack and cursed loudly.

As Bing stared at the sack of bones, it suddenly tilted forward. He wanted to get as far away from it as he could.

"Do you intend to wait for the next streetcar?" Bing asked worriedly.

"How else would we get home?"

"Let's start walking."

"Stupid fool! Do you know where we are?" Ba squatted and fanned himself furiously with his hat.

Bing pointed at Ba's bundle. "Both times, as soon as that sack of bones left the car, the electricity went right back on."

His father scowled.

"Fah! Those whites! They just don't want Chinese riding on their streetcars."

"But I've gone to Stanley Park and New Westminster on the streetcar with Uncle Jong and James. We never had any problems."

"Then the drivers on this route are bad ones."

"Wait and see," Bing said confidently. "As soon as we get on the next streetcar, the electricity will shut down. And then we'll get off, and the car will start up again. You'll see that I'm right!"

Ba shook his head and looked behind him, checking for the next streetcar.

"You're scared, that's all."

Bing turned away and trudged along the side of the road. He was right about the bones. He knew that for sure.

"Stupid fool, you're crazy, do you know that?" Ba shouted after him.

A streetcar appeared from the opposite direction, from downtown. It clanged its bell in warning and passed Bing with a swoosh. He didn't look up. He wanted to get away from his father and that sack of bones.

"Hey, wait for me," Ba called.

Bing marched on. He dragged the pickaxe over the grass alongside the road, but it became tangled in the weeds. The shovels banged painfully on his back. He rolled his shoulders and tried to shift the weight around. When his father's footsteps drew nearer, Bing crossed the road.

"Don't come near me!" he yelled. "I don't want to walk near you."

Ba cursed, but remained on the shadier side of the road, much to Bing's relief.

*Just keep those bones away from me,* he thought. *Something isn't right about them.*

Bing recalled another old Chinese ghost story:

> *Two young brothers were sent to fetch firewood one day. They had been told to return home early but had wasted time teasing worms from the damp ground.*
>
> *At dusk, a puppy ran by them. A girl with long hair came running after it.*
>
> *"Come back, you bad dog," she called. "Come back!"*
>
> *But the little dog ran into a graveyard. Every time its owner drew near, it darted away. She chased and chased it but fell and got dirty. The boys laughed and hooted at her.*
>
> *She gave them a pleading look. "Won't you help me?"*

*"What will you give us?" the boys replied.*

*The girl reached into her smock and held up two copper coins. Each boy grabbed one and started after the puppy. The dog raced around the mounds and the markers, and the brothers took care not to step on anything sacred. This made it harder to catch the dog, though finally they cornered it. But when they looked for the girl, she wasn't at the gate. They looked everywhere and called out for her. But she wasn't anywhere to be seen, so they let the dog go.*

*When the brothers told their mother about the coins, she told them to take the pennies and throw them back into the cemetery. But it was too late. The next day, the boys fell ill and died at the very same hour.*

"Hey, stupid fool. Hurry!" Ba's shouts pierced Bing's thoughts.

Bing glanced back and saw his father standing by a horse and wagon, waving his arms.

*What good fortune!* Bing thought.

It was Dent-head Fong, one of Uncle Won's drivers, sitting high behind Red Hare. Bing had privately named the horse after the loyal steed of Guan Gung, the God of War. Uncle Won and his men simply referred to the horses as *the black one, the short-tailed one* or *the one that limps.*

Ba lifted the sack of bones onto the wagon. He took the shovels from Bing and tossed them aboard. Then he bent close and whispered, "Don't tell Dent-head anything. Don't mention the streetcar. If he asks why we're walking, tell him you were carsick and couldn't stomach the ride."

Bing clambered onto the back as his father went to sit beside Dent-head. Ba had told many lies in his lifetime, but this was the first time he had instructed Bing to lie. Bing glanced at the sack of bones and shifted far away from it. Clearly, the bones were bothering Ba too.

# Chapter Three

B ING AND HIS FATHER OCCUPIED ONE OF FIVE NARROW ROOMS CRAMMED INTO THE SECOND STOREY OF UNCLE WON'S STORE, A CROWDED AND RICKETY BUILDING LIKE SO MANY OTHERS IN CHINATOWN.

The ground floor housed a huge counter where Uncle Won sweet-talked his customers and dispatched his wagons and drivers. A big calendar hung on the wall, as did several spring-loaded clipboards holding invoices, receipts and packing slips. There was also a potbelly stove surrounded by wooden chairs, wide shelves that ran to the ceiling and a large table where the men gathered for meals. In the summer, no one switched on the electric bulb because light streamed through the wide windows facing the street.

In the evenings, friends and acquaintances would drift in and discuss the day's events or read a Chinese newspaper, while others asked Uncle Won to read aloud a letter from home or to write to wives and family in China. Under a steamship ad tacked to the wall, Uncle Won had set up a cloth board. Pinned on it were letters sent from China to men who had once boarded at the store or had used its mailing address. Some envelopes had been there since Bing's arrival in Canada six years before. After he had learned to read English, Bing was able to decipher some of the handwriting. But now the ink was faded and the paper had dried and curled.

In Ba's room, one wall held homemade bunk beds and a lopsided tower of packing crates that formed shelves. Clothing, blankets, old newspapers and towels were crammed into them. In the corner lay a pile of tin cans, hand-tools and empty jars. The place was more like a hallway than a room. Still, this was the only place where Bing could practise boxing.

As soon as Ba went to the water closet to wash up for the evening meal, Bing kicked off his boots and took up a menacing stance. With his knees bent, he put up his fists and glared at his reflection in the mirror.

*Elbows bent and at my chest? Chin down? Right fist at eye level ready to block?* Bing circled an invisible challenger. *Left jab, right jab. Left hook, right hook.* He pictured his father's face and threw a solid uppercut. *No, no, not Ba,* he thought. Mother had ordered him to respect his father. *Better to practise on Freddie Cox's scrawny face.*

Bing moved his feet faster, shifting and shuffling from side to side. *One-two, one-two.* His shoulders ached, but he didn't stop throwing punches. *One-two, one-two.*

"What's this? Waltzing?"

Bing spun around and saw James grinning in the doorway. He cursed himself for not setting the lock.

James was five years older, taller and much stronger. He had finished school and now held a good job at the Bank of Vancouver. The two boys had met on the steamship coming to Canada. They spent six weeks together in steerage. When a bad storm howled over the heaving waves, the boys were seasick together. By the time the ship pulled into port, they were friends for life.

"Is that a new dance?" chuckled James, leaning against the wall and tipping a bottle of soda water into his mouth. "Is that what they teach at school now?"

Bing didn't answer.

"Looks like you're getting ready for a fight."

"What's it to you?"

"Who with?"

"Nobody you know. His name is Freddie Cox. He's trouble. Freddie failed grade five and Miss Cruikshank put him at the back with us Chinese. On the first day of class,

Freddie raised his hand and asked, *Can I sit somewhere else? It stinks back here.* I thought I had stepped in horse dung without noticing."

"That's because your nose is always filled with snot," James said with a grin, "and you can't smell anything."

Bing ignored the teasing.

"Then Miss Cruikshank slammed her ruler down on her desk and marched right back to where we sat. She wriggled her nose and said, *No Frederick, you're mistaken. There's nothing back here but the smell of failure.*

"Everyone laughed, and from then on Freddie started picking on me every single day. He jabbed me with his pencil, his ruler and his knuckles. He pushed me down the stairs and I cut my lip. After boxing classes, I was black with bruises, because he was my sparring partner."

"Is he bigger than you?"

"Yeah."

"So how will you fight him?"

Bing shrugged, so James changed the topic.

"How many bones did you find today?"

*A few hundred,* Bing was about to say, but Ba returned at that moment, wet hair plastered to his forehead and a towel around his waist. It was Bing's turn to go wash up for dinner, so James went downstairs. But when Bing returned from the water closet, Ba was nowhere to be seen. Bing went downstairs where the evening meal was being served, but was surprised to see that his father wasn't there either.

*Ba must have gone out,* Bing thought. *Good! Less trouble tonight.*

Ever since Ba had come back to Vancouver and moved into the store, the workers had been uneasy about eating with the bone collector. They thought he spread bad luck around. They even thought he carried the smell of death.

*Ba hasn't even told Mother or Grandmother about how he earns his living,* Bing thought as Uncle Sing brought platters of food in from the kitchen.

Uncle Won sat in his favourite chair and spooned soup from a tureen into his mouth.

"The front wheel of my wagon cracked," Big Ming declared, "and I had to wrap wire around it so I could wobble back to town. Took four hours instead of one."

"You're just slow and lazy," said white-haired Uncle Yung. He picked up his chopsticks. "Don't blame it on broken wheels."

Uncle Won waved his finger at Uncle Yung. "You were late getting back, too," he admonished.

"You won't believe what happened to me today!" exclaimed Uncle Yung. "I turned a curve and a wagon was coming at me. The road was narrow and only one team could pass. The other driver wouldn't back up and neither would I. Each of us waited for the other one to pull over first. Finally, another wagon pulled up behind the other team. It was two against one, so I had to back up."

"The customs inspector was doubly stupid today," said Dent-head Fong. He bent forward to sniff the serving plates of food. "He wouldn't let my horse move until I opened every crate. I wanted to tell him to go and jump in the harbour."

"That inspector is so fat!" Old Hoy chortled. "If he fell into the harbour, he'd float all the way to Vancouver Island and not even get cold!"

The men hooted and thumped their bowls hard on the table. Bing joined in the laughter. He wished he could ride the wagons with them and travel up and down the streets every day.

Uncle Sing pointed to Bing's plate. "I knew you would have a big appetite today, Bing," he said.

Bing gobbled up his food as fast as he could. There was juicy tomato and beef, omelettes with onions and roast pork and crunchy lotus root soup.

"Wah, sure smells good!" Ba said bursting through the front door.

He filled a bowl with rice and pulled up a chair. Abruptly, Old Hoy and Uncle Yung stood up. Hoy's chair crashed to the ground.

The two drivers marched to the front door and stomped out. Silence gripped the diners as Ba ignored the insult and shovelled rice into his mouth.

Dent-head glanced at Big Ming, who had resumed eating but more quickly now. All eyes were downcast. When Bing swallowed, the food stuck in his throat. The only sound was the rattle of wooden chopsticks against the earthenware bowls.

Uncle Won swallowed and then burped. "Tell your buddies they can go work somewhere else if they don't approve of who boards in my store. The bone collector can live here as long as he wants," he said loudly to the workers who stayed behind. "Besides, what's there to fear?"

"They're afraid of ghosts invading their bodies and making them sick, that's what!" Uncle Sing snorted.

"Fah!" Ba dismissed him with a flick of his hand. "There's more danger from white thugs wanting to brawl on the streets than ghosts."

"You don't believe in ghosts?" Dent-head asked.

"I've dug up hundreds of sets of bones, and no ghost has ever bothered me," Ba said.

"You're a good man. No ghost would dare bother you. That's why the Council selected you to collect bones. Maybe there's something we can learn from you," Uncle Won said.

*Good man? Hardly,* Bing thought, while he chewed his food. *When other villagers received money from their Gold Mountain men, Mother and Grandmother had to lie about having enough to last a year. If Ba was such a good man, why hadn't he told Mother and Grandmother he was planning to come back to China for a visit, instead of turning up in our village unannounced? Why hadn't he brought back gifts for everyone when he did return? Mother and Grandmother had to lie about his failures in order to save face for the family. Ba even tricked me into coming back with him to Canada. He promised I would have fresh chicken to eat every day, tall horses to ride and great buildings fifteen storeys high to visit.*

"What about you, Bing?" asked Uncle Won. "Did you see anything strange today?"

"No," replied Bing picking at the blisters on his hands. He wanted to be left alone. He wanted to forget about the graveyard.

Ba lifted one foot onto his chair and rubbed his calf. His hands were dark and rough as tree bark, especially against the pale skin of his leg.

"We dug up Shum's bones. He died almost ten years ago. Ever hear of him?"

"So long ago? I wasn't here then!" Big Ming shook his head and kept on eating.

"Not many people with that name," commented Uncle Sing.

*Tell them the bones had no skull,* Bing thought. *Otherwise they won't help you. Those bones are dangerous! They stopped two streetcars!*

"I hear there was a fire on Shanghai Street last night," Uncle Sing said.

"I didn't hear the fire wagons," Uncle Won replied.

"Fire wagons will come *here*," a gruff voice at the door cut in, "if I don't get my money soon!"

Broken-leg, one of Loan Shark's ugliest thugs, limped toward the table.

"Hey, Old Chan, you still owe money. The boss wants payment."

"Soon," Ba said spitting into a spittoon.

"You said that six months ago." Broken-leg's sleeveless vest revealed his enormous arms, thick and solid with muscle.

One huge fist nudged Ba. "Didn't you just finish a job up north? Where's the money?"

"Sent it home to China."

"Liar! You stopped and gambled in every town along the way."

Ba glanced at Bing and then at the debt collector. "Tell your boss he'll get paid soon enough," said Ba.

Broken-leg slowly rubbed his great forehead, smooth and round as a melon. It glistened with sweat and oil. It was rumoured that he killed people by ramming his head between their eyes.

Broken-leg flexed his hands and grinned. "Hey, Tin-brother." He used Ba's first name and added 'brother' to suggest they shared something in common. "I'm just a middleman, come to deliver a message. No need to get rude."

"You're the rude one," Ba snapped. "You're interrupting our meal."

"You never learn, do you?" Broken-leg snorted. "You can't escape a debt. The boss always recovers his money, one way or another. Even if you sprout wings, you can't escape."

Then he slapped Ba hard on the back and lumbered out the front door.

Bing swallowed nervously. If Broken-leg had wanted, he could have squashed Ba flat as a dishrag and wrung him out to dry.

Gambling halls outnumbered restaurants in Chinatown, where everyone gambled late into the night. Most men retreated from the tables when their last penny left their fingers, but not Ba. He wheedled money from friends and acquaintances. And when his losing streak continued, he went to Loan Shark and borrowed more money. No one felt sorry for him.

"What were you saying about a fire?" Uncle Won asked Uncle Sing.

"Fat Old Wong doused it himself. Ran out with a blanket and smothered the flames."

"White boys?"

"Of course! But no one knows for sure. No one saw anything."

"Fat Old Wong shouldn't leave crates outside. Anyone can toss in a match or a cigarette."

"Did you hear what happened to Drip-lip Wing?" Uncle Sing asked.

"No," replied Uncle Won.

"He was attacked; seized from behind while coming home from work. Every time he shouted for help, he was kicked in the mouth."

"Terrible! It's become worse. Old Ouyang had his shoulder dislocated by white boys. They grabbed his pigtail and took sixteen dollars from him—two whole weeks of wages!"

"We have to do more to protect ourselves," Big Ming said.

"We need to protect the horses too," Dent-head added.

"Wah, what tasty food!" crowed Lee Dat, strolling in with a big smile. He was a job contractor who handled Chinese labour for logging camps, sawmills, steamships and canneries. "I should have come here earlier!"

He beckoned to Bing. "Hey, Bing-wing, I found a job for you."

"Me?"

"Didn't your Uncle Sing tell you? He asked me to find you a job."

When Bing glanced over, Uncle Sing grinned back. But Ba glared at him.

Bing faced Lee Dat and asked, "Where?"

"In a big house. There's a family that needs a houseboy."

"Is the boy old enough to work outside Chinatown?" Uncle Won frowned.

"What does it pay?" Bing wanted to make sure this was a serious proposition.

"Five dollars a week."

"When does it start?"

"Tomorrow."

"Perfect!" cried Bing. "Is it far away?"

"Not far at all. Just across the water, on Fairview." He pronounced it, *Feh-will*.

"I think he should stay behind and work with his father," Uncle Won said. "That way, he won't get into trouble."

Under the table, Bing tugged at Uncle Sing's sleeve, hoping he wouldn't mention the time Bing had been caught in the coal yards where no children were allowed, or the time a policeman had brought him home. On that day, the drivers had rushed him to the hospital, thinking he had a broken arm.

"You'll get a room of your own, a bed and three meals a day," Lee Dat explained. "And Sunday afternoons are free, so you can come home."

*Three meals? We only get two here.*

"Which house?"

"Where Yawn-mouth Yuen was."

"No wonder you're dumping it on the boy!" Uncle Won exclaimed. "No one else wants that job. You've been trying to fill that job for a week. Yawn-mouth Yuen quit because that house has ghosts!"

Bing began to have second thoughts about the job. The offer didn't seem so attractive any more.

"Fah, Yawn-mouth is a lazy worm and drinks too much whiskey," Lee Dat answered.

"You say he was lying?" asked Uncle Won.

"He never mentioned ghosts to me. And he worked in that house for three years." Lee Dat strode over to the spittoon and spat. "They probably fired him for not doing his job. He was probably trying to save face with that tale about ghosts."

Uncle Sing nudged Bing.

"Hey, are you afraid of ghosts, Bing?"

"Afraid?" Ba leapt up. "This one runs away from his own shadow! At the cemetery today, his shovel nicked a rock, and he ran like a fox from the hen coop."

Ba crouched behind a chair to continue. "This is how he reacts to a rock. Runs and hides as if the farmer's wife is chasing him with an axe. Whenever I found bones, he wouldn't come near them."

Bing wanted to run from the room. But if he did, the men would know he was afraid.

"And when he finally did pick up a bone, he dropped it like a boiled egg just out of the pot!"

Ba turned his face toward his son and rolled a toothpick from one side of his mouth to the other.

"Are you going to stay and work with family, or are you striking out on your own?"

The men stared at Bing, waiting. He had no desire to dig up graves or to work beside his father.

*But what if that house was truly haunted?* he thought. *I'd run away and Lee Dat would hear about it. Then everyone in Chinatown would call me a coward.*

Bing opened his mouth, but no sound came out.

"Wait!" Uncle Sing raised his hand. "Yawn-mouth told me something else. Isn't that the house of the man who fights? Remember two years ago when they erected a tent in the drill grounds and charged money to see two men wearing short pants dance around and hit each other?"

"I don't know anything about that." Lee Dat shrugged.

"What's the name of that family?" asked Uncle Won. Sometimes he read the English newspapers.

"Bun-lee."

Bing's eyes widened. That would be Bulldog Bentley, the city champ! At school, Bulldog had visited Bing's athletics class to teach boxing, a welcome change from the military drilling and marching. The boxer was a head shorter than their instructor Major Lundy was, but Bulldog's feet had moved so quickly that the Major looked plodding. Then, Bulldog landed a solid punch on the Major's chin. He teetered and almost stumbled to the ground. All the boys cheered and Bulldog grinned.

After the boxing session, Major Lundy advised the boys to follow Bulldog's career in the newspapers. Some of them brought in clippings with ink drawings that highlighted Bulldog's wins, his trophies and his trips to boxing matches in America and Europe. One article named Bulldog as the city's conquering hero, under a headline proclaiming *Native Son Soars to New Heights*.

Ba flicked his toothpick into the spittoon.

"Better look elsewhere for the donkey you need," he said to Lee Dat. "This son of mine is scared of ghosts."

*I wonder if Bulldog would teach me to box.* The thought set Bing's heart racing.

The job contractor turned to go. "Oh well, there are always people looking for work."

"Wait!" Bing called. "I'll take the job!"

*A boxer like Bulldog Bentley wouldn't live in a haunted house. Lee Dat must be right about Yawn-mouth telling lies to cover up his own laziness.*

"Good," Lee Dat grinned. "I'll take you over there tomorrow morning. Do you have clean clothes?"

"I'll wash these tonight," offered Bing.

The contractor made a face.

"You can't walk into a nice house looking like a beggar. You have to buy some new clothes."

Bing looked at his father, but there was no response. The man didn't have a penny to his name.

"Tin-brother, I'll lend Bing some money," Uncle Sing said. "He can go buy some clothes from Uncle Jong. This job is a good opportunity for him to learn about the white man's world."

"Thank you, Uncle Sing," Bing said. But then his stomach tightened.

*What have I got myself into?* he thought.

# Chapter Four

THE DELICIOUS SMELL OF FRIED FOOD WAFTED OUT OF THE RESTAURANTS AS BING DARTED DOWN THE WOODEN SIDEWALKS OF CHINATOWN. DINNERTIME WAS THE BUSIEST TIME AS MEN ON THEIR WAY HOME FROM WORK STOPPED AT THE BUTCHERS AND THE GREENGROCERS.

"Fresh *bok-choy*! Tender *gai-lan*! Juicy tomatoes. Get them here!"

A fishmonger stood next to a barrel of live fish, sharpening his knife blade. A shopper, with Chinese sausages slung over his shoulder and a chunk of pork dangling from a waxed string, pushed past Bing.

Bing burst into James' home, one of Chinatown's sewing factories. In the front of the store, two rows of foot-powered sewing machines were silent now. They seemed harmless, but their needles could pierce flesh and bone so cleanly that no pain was felt until bright red blood spurted out.

James sat with his father and mother at the back of the shop eating dinner.

"Ah, Bing-wing," James' mother, Auntie Jong, called out, "have you eaten yet? Come and join us!"

"Thank you, Auntie, but I've just come from dinner," Bing smiled. Close up, she smelled of flower water, a scent that reminded him of his mother.

"Hey, is that money I see in your hand?" asked James.

"I've come here to buy new clothes. I got a job!"

"No!" James looked astounded. "Where?"

"I'm going to be a houseboy in Fairview."

Auntie Jong motioned him to sit and join them.

"Houseboy?" exclaimed James. "You don't want that, Bing. That was my first job, and I hated it. It's the worst job in the world! The employers think they own you. You wake up before them and go to bed after them. You work every single minute of the day, except when you're using the water closet."

"I forgot about your houseboy job." It was only recently that James' fluent English had got him a job at the bank.

"When Dent-head Fong worked as a houseboy," James' father, Uncle Jong, added, "he had to iron the newspapers each morning before the lady of the house would read them. Can you believe such foolishness? If he singed a single page, he was scolded in front of the entire family."

"What about Little Loo?" said James. "They accused him of stealing, and the police came and handcuffed him. He was released from jail a day later, but no one ever apologized."

"Are there children in the house?" asked Auntie Jong.

"I don't know," replied Bing.

"You should have asked before you took the job," said James. "There's no fate worse than a large family with small children. There's less to eat, double the amount of work, and you get no respect at all from the children. Being a houseboy isn't a job; it's a punishment!"

"When the young Miss set fire to the nursery," Uncle Jong continued, "Little Loo knew the young Miss' parents would side with her; so he went along with the girl's lies, accepted the blame and had to pay for the damage."

"Oh, stop tormenting the boy," said Auntie Jong. She smiled warmly at Bing and put one hand on his shoulder. "He's worried enough about going outside of Chinatown to earn money. Everyone has to start somewhere, isn't that so?"

"Yawn-mouth Yuen had the job before me," Bing said.

"Didn't he quit because the house has ghosts?" James asked.

"No!" Auntie Jong's hands flew to her face. "What will you do?"

"I'm sure Yawn-mouth is lying," Bing said. "The house can't be haunted. A boxing champion lives there. He came to my school once. Maybe he'll teach me how to fight better."

"But you're only the houseboy. You're a servant and Chinese."

"But he taught everyone how to fight in our athletics class."

"That was different. Besides, boxers can't fight ghosts."

"Ba says there's no such thing as ghosts."

"And since when do you listen to your father?"

Bing shrugged. He had often wished Ba were more like James' father. Whenever Bing helped Uncle Jong put together a rush order of pants, Uncle Jong would joke, "Hey, I owe you wages. I'll mark it in the account book. Shall I pay you in cash or candy?"

Uncle Jong rummaged through the shelves of finished garments and brought over a four-button jacket, long pants, a white shirt and black stockings.

"See if these fit."

James leaned forward and said, "Maybe you should go to church and get protection from the white man's God and His angels."

"Maybe you'd better learn to sing hymns and pray like the white people," Uncle Jong piped in.

"Don't make fun of others." Auntie Jong hushed them with a disapproving look. "You two think you know everything!"

"What if I don't get enough to eat at that house?" Bing asked.

"Sneak into the pantry in the middle of the night and steal ham and bread," James replied.

"What if they lock the breadbox?"

"Bring dried beef with you and hide it under your pillow."

"What if the mice eat it all up?"

"Put it in a tin box."

"A boy so young shouldn't go to a house with that kind of a reputation," murmured Auntie as she stood up to stack the empty bowls.

"Here's an idea!" James exclaimed. He slammed his hand on the table. "I'll take Bing to Fortuneteller."

"Then take him before it gets dark," said Auntie.

"C'mon, Bing. Fortuneteller will know what you should do if there are ghosts in that house."

As the two friends burst into the still warm evening, music from a Chinese opera floated out from the Sing Wah Theatre.

Bing pressed the bundle of new clothes tightly to his chest and asked, "Who is Fortuneteller?"

"A wise old man."

"Does he have powerful charms?"

"Yes, lots of people go to him for them."

"Have you?"

James didn't answer. Instead, he led the way to the Kwong Yuen store, one of the largest establishments in Chinatown, where men boarded in rooms just like those at Uncle Won's. A rowdy game of *Heavenly Nines* clattered in the main hall, with men shouting and shrieking each time a domino tile hit the table. The sweet smell of tobacco hung in the air and rose from the water pipes the men were smoking. The second floor had more than a dozen doors that lined the hallway, but James knew exactly where to knock.

"Who is it?" called a gruff voice.

"Your good friend," replied James.

The door swung open to a haze of incense. In the room, a Chinese scroll covered one wall. On the other side of the room was a porcelain statue of Guan Gung. The statue stood tall and straight, with battle armour on his right side and a green scholar's robe on his left. His black beard hung long from his dark red face. On his head was a helmet crowned with a great red stone. Beneath him, a narrow altar table held plates of fresh fruit, tiny wine cups, red candles in carved holders and a gleaming brass urn.

Fortuneteller wore a collarless Chinese shirt with loose sleeves and buttons made from rolled cloth. His forehead was shaved, his pigtail was white, his eyebrows were bushy and wisps of beard dangled from his chin. Bing had never seen him before.

Fortuneteller shuffled past them to a desk crowded with ink-stones, paper and writing brushes. He slowly lowered himself into a sagging rattan chair.

"So, young man, what do you want now?" He spoke in an unfamiliar dialect, and Bing had to concentrate in order to understand what he said.

"My friend wants to ask a question," James said.

"He wants his fortune told? He'll have to pay."

"I can give you clothes from my father's factory," said James, but the old man snorted in refusal.

Bing stared at a wall chart showing a human face covered with dotted lines and Chinese characters. "I don't want a reading," he declared, "but I can pay for your help."

"You have money?" The old man looked surprised.

"Yes, I'm starting work tomorrow as a houseboy," Bing said proudly, showing off his new clothes.

"Ah," remarked Fortuneteller.

"But people say the house is haunted."

"Oh. And do you believe them?"

Bing shrugged.

"Some people say they've never seen a ghost," said Fortuneteller. "But others swear they have. They have encountered the faces of people they knew and those of total strangers. Have you ever met a ghost?"

Bing shook his head.

"And Chan Tin is your father?" Fortuneteller asked.

"How did you know?"

"I know everything," the old man sniffed.

"My father doesn't believe in ghosts."

"Then why did you come here?"

"It was my idea," explained James. "I thought you could help him."

"Ah, this young man works outside Chinatown and is full of wisdom." Fortuneteller stroked his whiskers and then leaned forward. "Bing-wing, you're young and haven't seen much. The world is filled with all kinds of people and unfamiliar events you must face in order to become an adult. You're still a child; there's much for you to learn."

Bing resented being called *a child*. "I just want to know what to do if I see a ghost."

The old man shrugged. "Are you afraid of ghosts?"

"No, but I have to know what to do in case I see one."

"Talk to it and ask what it wants. All ghosts have a reason for coming back."

"I won't talk to a ghost!"

"You said you weren't afraid," Fortuneteller chided. "Have you heard this chant before?

*He who does only right,*
*Will never ever know fright.*
*Not even from rapping at the door,*
*At three in the morning or at four."*

"I've heard it a hundred times," Bing said impatiently. "Can you sell me a charm to keep ghosts away?"

The old man shook his head.

"Not even for an emergency?"

"Little One, you're going to work for Westerners. My charms have never been tested on white spirits."

"Then here's your chance. If it works, you'll win new customers from all over the city!"

"You're stubborn, aren't you?" The old man chuckled. "You'll make a fine businessman one day."

"Can you give me a picture of Guan Gung?"

Fortuneteller recoiled as if he had been insulted.

"Guan Gung is the most powerful of our gods. He is not for children!"

"So what can you give me?"

The old man began to say something but then reached across the table to a bowl of stones. He paused thoughtfully before picking one out. "Keep this in your pocket. Hold it tight in times of need."

The stone was smooth and round, like ocean rocks that had been washed onto the beach. It was speckled black and white with a slash of rusty brown cutting through it. Bing sniffed at it but smelled only the incense that clouded the room. He flipped the stone upside down, but no secret codes or spells were written on it. When Bing hefted it, the stone felt heavy and solid. But there was nothing special about it.

"Can I have another one for my father?"

Bing wanted a protective charm for Ba too, just in case the headless set of bones caused more trouble. Before Bing left China, Grandmother had asked him to take care of Ba.

But before he had a chance to answer Bing's request, Fortuneteller's head rolled back, his mouth fell open and he began to snore.

As the two friends descended the stairs, James asked, "Why did you want to get a stone for your father? He's not afraid."

"Promise not to tell?"

James nodded and Bing described how Shum's bones had stalled the streetcars on the way back from the cemetery. Then he told James about the missing skull.

"Wah, that's strange!" James whistled and shook his head. "Even criminals who are executed get buried with their heads! You're lucky you don't have to handle bones any more. Your new job is far from the cemetery. And now you even have a charm to protect you, so you have nothing to worry about," he said, slapping Bing on the back.

"Nothing at all," Bing responded.

"Speaking of headless ghosts, did you ever hear the story about the scholar in the forest?"

Bing didn't want to hear a ghost story. But if he refused, his friend would know he was scared.

"Let's sit and I'll tell you," James said as they approached a hitching-bar.

*As a young scholar was travelling to the provincial capital one afternoon, he came to a roadside tea-stand at the entrance to a forest.*

*"Don't go into the forest so late in the day. It's haunted," the proprietor said.*

*But the scholar didn't believe in ghosts and entered the forest anyway.*

*When it grew dark, he relied on the bright moonlight to stay on the path. He soon grew weary and was pleased to find an inn, located by a bridge over the river. He ordered food, rented a room and slept very well that night. He dreamed of a beautiful song-girl with long shiny hair who came into his room and sang him to sleep.*

*The next morning, he resumed his journey and soon left the forest behind. When he arrived in the next town, he went to breakfast at a teahouse.*

*There, he noticed townspeople crowding around a table. Curious, the scholar pushed his way in and listened as a wide-eyed farmer recounted his tale.*

*"Last night I stopped in the forest to rest and fell asleep by the bridge. I was awakened by a woman's singing. In the moonlight, I saw a beautiful young woman walk from the bridge to the riverbank and kneel, as if to drink. Instead, she raised her arms, lifted her head off her shoulders and set it on top of the water. When she began washing the long strands of her hair, I ran for my life."*

*The scholar started trembling. Not knowing what to think, he went back to the bridge. When he arrived, there was no inn, just a freshly dug grave bearing the name of a young girl. Two days later, the young man fell ill. Nothing the doctors did could save him, and he died.*

"Are you trying to scare me?" Bing asked.

"No, but you should be careful," James said. "There's no telling what may happen to you outside Chinatown."

Then he gave Bing a brotherly slap on the back, got up and headed home.

Bing swallowed hard and started to walk back to Uncle Won's place.

*If only I were back in China! Then I wouldn't be afraid,* he thought. *Grandmother and Mother would go to the temple and pray. And the ancient gods and spirits would protect me. But here in Canada, who knows what works and what doesn't work? There is no one here I can rely on. But I won't allow myself to become afraid. Mother and Grandmother don't want me to be scared!*

This was the New World, the 20th century, the age of progress. Electric lights banished the dark, telephone wires carried human conversations over vast distances and moving pictures played on wide screens in the nickelodeons. What had once seemed like fantasy was now real. American inventors flew their machines into the air like birds and motorcars outran racehorses across the desert. Fortuneteller and his charms, Ba digging up human bones to send to China—these were all ancient superstitions. And Bing wanted to leave them far behind.

But all the same, Bing clutched the stone in his pocket and thought, *It's good to have some magic just in case.*

# A Ghost in the House

# Chapter Five

THE BRIGHT MORNING SUN STREAMED IN THROUGH THE OPEN WINDOW AT UNCLE WON'S. BING WOKE UP AND HEARD THE CITY STIRRING. DELIVERY WAGONS CLATTERED. HORSES CLIP-CLOPPED. STREETCARS SQUEALED. WATER SPLASHED ONTO THE STREET. SEAGULLS SCREECHED IN NEARBY FALSE CREEK.

Bing lay in bed imagining what Boxer Bentley's mansion might look like. It stood high on a hill surrounded by tall trees. A long, winding drive led up to a whitewashed veranda with columns. Suddenly, a headless skeleton emerged from a broken window on the second floor. Bing shuddered, afraid that the images he saw might be real. His hand groped under his pillow for Fortuneteller's stone.

Bing rolled to the edge of his bed and hung over the top bunk. The thin sheet on the bed below was neatly folded. His father had not slept there the night before.

*Maybe the graveyard ghost reached out from the shadows and swallowed him up,* thought Bing. *No, he's probably asleep on the floor of some gambling club.*

A fist pounded the door and Big Ming called out, "Hey, Little One, it's your turn to use the water closet!"

"Coming!" Bing replied, leaping to the ground.

When he finished, he went into the back courtyard to do his morning chores. The smell of animals and damp straw reminded him of his life in China: snorting pigs penned by the house, Grandmother feeding the chickens pecking in the stone courtyard and Mother sweeping up the kitchen with a broom.

As Bing tended to the horses, he thought of Shum's bones in the shed nearby. He kept a nervous eye on the shed door while he filled a pail with water.

*Those bones are powerful enough to halt electric streetcars. No telling what else they can do.*

Bing scattered the wet straw to dry, scrubbed the stalls with a wide broom and swept the dirty water out into the courtyard and toward the alley. Then, he fondly stroked the muzzle of Red Hare.

"I'm going away, my friend," he whispered. "Someone else will bring you food and water. I'll see you on Sundays."

After Bing poured pails of oats and water into the troughs, he went back into the store for breakfast. Uncle Won was at work already, writing with brush and black ink and clicking wooden beads on the abacus. At the nearby table, a tureen of soup and a platter of steamed salted meat were being served.

Old Hoy spooned hot broth into a bowl, complaining loudly about his aching gums. When Uncle Won left the room, Old Hoy frowned at Bing, "Where's your father?"

"Don't know."

"Can't the bone collector go somewhere else to sleep?" Old Hoy muttered.

"He's from the boss's village," Uncle Yung whispered. "How could he refuse to help?"

Bing pretended not to hear and wished Uncle Won would return. But Uncle Won remained out back. So Bing shovelled the rest of the rice into his mouth, took his empty bowl into the kitchen and ran upstairs to change into his new clothes. The shirt was stiff and the pants held a sharp crease. With a new cap on his head, he looked like the son of a wealthy merchant family. After Bing cleaned and shined up his old shoes, they looked like new.

Then Bing reached for Fortuneteller's stone and took a long look around the room. He felt as if he were about to cross an ocean, never to return.

Just as Bing came downstairs, the front door opened and Uncle Yung exclaimed, "Fah! The bone collector is back!"

Ba leaned against the door and clutched its frame. One hand was tucked into his waistband, his wrist wrapped in bandages. A purple bruise spread from his right eye toward one ear and the other side of his face revealed two broad cuts. One leg was oddly twisted, and his jacket pocket was torn.

Bing watched as the drivers helped his father limp to an empty chair.

"The police are useless," declared Dent-head. "We need to teach those hoodlums a lesson."

"Sooner or later, someone will die," shouted Old Hoy. "And we'll have to take matters into our own hands. The whites think we're cowards, but they're the ones who travel in gangs. We're not afraid of them."

"I've got a cudgel under my bed," said Uncle Yung.

Bing was silent. He'd heard their bold words and brave talk on other occasions but had never seen them take any action. The drivers were strong from lifting crates, but had they ever learned the martial arts? The only fighting he had seen in Chinatown was on stage when the opera troupe performed.

Bing had heard stories about Chinese heroes and heroines who fled to the mountains to escape persecution. There, protected from pursuers by great heights and thick mists, they learned fighting skills from the grand masters. When the fugitives had mastered the martial arts, they returned to defeat their enemies.

"No," Ba wheezed. "You've got it all wrong. White boys didn't do this. Loan Shark's thugs trapped me in the alley. It's not serious; just looks bad."

Any sympathy for Ba instantly disappeared. Muttering and grumbling, the men sauntered to the kitchen sink with their empty bowls.

"Get me some rice," he snapped at Bing.

Bing obeyed, and then watched Ba use one hand to fill his mouth, slurping noisily.

"Did Broken-leg do this to you?" Bing asked.

His father ignored him.

"How will you be able to work now?" Bing continued.

"Fah, don't mind me! I can take care of myself," Ba grunted, as he shoved the food in between his teeth.

"You should rebury Shum's bones in the graveyard," said Bing. "It's not good to keep them here."

"What! Are you scared of some stupid bones?" Ba threw down his spoon. "Stop nagging me, you stupid fool! Get to your houseboy job and let me tend to my bones! Don't you think I know how to do my job? I don't need you poking into my affairs. You'll have plenty of your own problems working for white people."

# Chapter Six

As the streetcar rumbled over the Westminster Street Bridge, Bing sat quietly beside Lee Dat and gazed out the window. A tugboat steamed by, towing a log-boom toward one of the False Creek sawmills. To the west, the wind dispersed the sawmills' smoke. On days like this, he could stand on the Chinatown side of False Creek and see Fairview. Its ridge formed the southern horizon beyond which lay the United States.

"Scared?" Lee Dat nudged Bing.

"Ba and I don't believe in ghosts."

"Who's talking about ghosts?" Lee Dat bounced a knuckle off Bing's forehead. "I'm asking you about moving to the big house."

"No, I'm not afraid of that."

At Seventh Avenue, Bing and Lee Dat got off and started walking. "The house isn't really that far from Chinatown," Lee Dat said. "If need be, you can walk home and save a nickel."

Bing looked around at the roads that had been cut through the forest. There were wooden sidewalks on only one side of the street, since the district wasn't finished yet. The houses looked freshly painted and their sharply sloped roofs were trimmed with gingerbread. They passed mansions with steeples and chimneys poking into the skyline. Nearby trees were so tall and thick that it would take six men with their arms outstretched to encircle their trunks. In some places the underbrush, fallen logs and bramble made the forest impassable.

Bing lagged behind, taking in the surroundings.

"Hurry, your boss is waiting!" called Lee Dat. He stopped and turned his body to shield a match from the wind as he lit a cigar. "We're here."

When Bing caught up with Lee Dat, the contractor spun him around.

"Over there!" he said, pointing to a house set behind a grand lawn.

*How could such a magnificent house be haunted?* Bing wondered.

The foundation was stone, every block identical in size, like squares of a checkerboard. Bing marvelled at the time and money that would have been needed just to cut the stone. The house was five or six times wider than any building in Chinatown and had ten times as many windows. A porch big enough for a family picnic surrounded the front door. Above it, a second floor balcony curved around the front. Three massive chimneys jutted into the sky.

"Are there children in this family?" Bing asked.

"Just a baby, still drinking his mother's milk."

They walked past fruit trees, sculptured shrubs and flowerbeds. Long tangles of red and yellow roses hung from trellises.

Lee Dat led Bing to the rear entrance of the house.

Bing hesitated.

"It's not because we're Chinese," Lee Dat said. "Fah, don't make that face. Only the owners and their guests use the front door. All groceries, deliveries and servants come to the back entrance."

"I never made a face," Bing protested, licking his palm and flattening his hair.

"Fah, don't lie to me! You children think you're smart because you speak English. But you're still Chinese."

*You grown-ups think you know everything,* Bing thought. *But you don't.*

Lee Dat knocked and a short woman, round as a barrel, threw open the door.

"Say hello to Mrs. Moore," said Lee Dat, gesturing to the woman, who had her hands on her hips.

Mrs. Moore's brown hair was set in a bun at the top of her head and stray strands dangled loose. An apron covered her uniform and a silver crucifix hung on a chain that dangled from her neck. Her wide, fleshy face was bright pink, and Bing felt her stern gaze dart up and down him.

"He's so small," she trilled. "Does he speak English? Has he ever done housework?"

Bing panicked. He had scrubbed more horses and stable stalls than hallways and parlours. Nobody at Uncle Won's store ever did housework. Four times a year, they moved the furniture and mopped the floors. Bing should have realized that employers preferred experienced workers. Even Uncle Won complained about the mistakes of new drivers. Bing worried about making a fool of himself.

The housekeeper fanned Lee Dat's cigar smoke away from her face.

"Weren't there any young women from Chinatown you could bring me? Girls know how to wash dishes and sweep."

"I know how to use a broom," Bing blurted, without mentioning that it usually dripped black with stable muck.

Mrs. Moore's eyebrows arched. "Well, at least he speaks good English," she said, quickly turning around and stepping back inside the house.

*For someone so plump, she's surprisingly quick,* Bing thought.

"Don't drag your feet, boy. Let's get to work," Mrs. Moore said as Bing began to follow her through the doorway.

But Lee Dat grabbed Bing's arm. "Whatever the old lady says, you do it. This is a job, and you're getting paid. Follow her orders, learn all you can and mind every detail. Understand?"

Bing shook him off and stepped into the kitchen. It was filled with the sweet smell of sugar being cooked. He saw tall shelves that must have contained table settings for fifty people. A porcelain sink stretched longer than the water trough in Uncle Won's stable. Two shiny faucets were mounted high above it. Clamped to the long table were two meat grinders, each with a funnel at the top and a handle at the side. The kitchen was hot and smoky.

*I hope the soot doesn't soil my new clothes,* Bing thought.

"I'll show you around the house, young man," Mrs. Moore said, tying on a fresh apron. "Then we have to make lunch for Mrs. Bentley. Watch carefully, boy, because in future you'll be the one setting the table and serving the meals. Understand?"

"Yes, Ma'am."

The next room contained wooden chairs with soft seats, a chandelier of crystal teardrops and a huge table that could have accommodated Bing's entire class for a meal. Great paintings in ornate frames hung on the walls.

"Dining room," Mrs. Moore said, as she strode into an alcove of large windows with three wingback chairs facing the garden.

"Conservatory," she said as she continued the tour of the house.

But Bing couldn't understand the name of the room. "Beg pardon?" he asked.

*Did she say cemetery?* he thought.

"Con-ser-va-tory," Mrs. Moore repeated.

When someone knocked loudly at the back door, Mrs. Moore pulled out a timepiece and glanced at it.

"It's the laundry delivery. You wait right here."

After she left, Bing cautiously stepped into the front parlour. It was large but crowded with upholstered chairs and small rugs, lamps with fringed shades, a well-polished piano and several bookcases filled to capacity. Bing didn't dare touch anything. The chairs were covered with lace damask and strewn with satin-bound cushions. The fireplace was big enough to roast a large pig.

The heavy footsteps of a man sounded in the hallway above, and Bing ducked into the nearest corner by a front window. As the footsteps came down the stairs, they were followed by the lighter steps of a woman. Then Bing heard a familiar voice. It was Bulldog Bentley, sounding weary and exasperated.

"Dearest, I'm sorry, but I have to leave. There's no need to fret. Gerald Rogers is my good friend, and he'll sell the house for you in no time."

Bing wanted to jump out and greet Bulldog.

*That must be Mrs. Bentley with him,* Bing thought. *I'd better not disturb them.*

"It's been over two weeks already," Mrs. Bentley said. "I hope you didn't tell him anything about the goings-on."

"I didn't say anything," Bulldog continued. "You can tell him whatever you want. "

"I don't know what I should say." The woman's tone sounded edgy.

"Remember, selling this place was your idea."

Bing swallowed hard. His hands were cold, just like the times when he had overheard his parents arguing, or when Grandmother and Mother had shouted at one other.

"Wait just a minute! Don't blame me for anything. We both agreed that moving to Toronto would be best for the family. You need a real job."

"Boxing *is* a real job. And Vancouver is my home!"

A tense pause charged the atmosphere.

Then Bulldog's wife asked softly, "Do you wish you had married someone else?"

Bulldog sighed before replying.

"No, no. You know what's good for all of us and I don't. You're my best girl. You think of my best interests. I know I won't be able to box all my life."

When Mrs. Bentley answered, she sounded happier. "My father will be delighted to have you working with him in Toronto."

There was a knock at the front door.

"I'll be right there," Bulldog called out. Then, in a quieter voice, he said, "Darling, I wish I could stay and help you sell the house. But you know this boxing tour was planned a long time ago."

"It's just a matter of proper organization," she said brightly. "We've finally hired a new houseboy. As soon as the house is sold, I'll get him to start packing."

"I have to go, or I'll miss my train. The carriage is waiting."

When the door shut, Bing held his breath. *What if Mrs. Bentley walks into the parlour and finds me hiding here?*

From the kitchen came the sound of a door opening and closing.

Then Mrs. Bentley started up the stairs and called out, "Mrs. Moore! Mr. Bentley has left on his tour."

"May he come home safely," Mrs. Moore called back.

Bing fled into the conservatory and groaned with dismay.

*If Bulldog's gone on a boxing tour, that means no boxing lessons for me! And if Mrs. Bentley's going to sell the house, that means I'll lose my job!* Then a darker thought occurred to Bing. *What if Mrs. Bentley wants to move because the house really is haunted, and she's too scared to live here? What if Yawn-mouth Yuen is telling the truth?*

Bing visualized himself running out of the house after Lee Dat shouting, *"Wait for me! I don't want this job! I've changed my mind."*

"You'll be dusting this afternoon." Mrs. Moore strode in and interrupted his worrisome daydream. "We're long overdue for a good cleaning. In summer, we leave the windows open and plenty of dust sneaks in. But first, follow me."

They climbed the dimly lit rear stairs, narrow and bare of carpeting. On the second floor, the doors they passed were tightly closed, as if concealing secrets. The hardwood floor creaked here and there.

The housekeeper pointed at one door and said, "That's Mr. and Mrs. Bentley's bedroom. I'll take you in when Mrs. Bentley isn't here."

Bing nodded.

Mrs. Moore went to another door and opened it. "This is the water closet."

Bing peeked in. A great bathing tub was set on eagle claw legs, surrounded by a large folding screen, a wooden commode and a washstand. A window let in light through lace curtains and the tile floor shone. Back at Uncle Won's, the water closet had a wooden floor that was always wet.

Mrs. Moore walked into another room across the hall. Bing saw a sparsely furnished bedroom with bed, dresser, lamps and a washstand.

"This room is for guests," Mrs. Moore explained. "Mrs. Bentley often has relatives visiting from out of town."

In the next room, the walls were lined with bookcases and framed certificates. It looked cozy, but Bing recoiled as if he had just stepped outside into the cold air on a winter day. Instinctively, his hand gripped Fortuneteller's stone. As he passed a writing desk, his other hand brushed the tabletop. The wood felt like ice.

*This is summer and it's almost noon. No room should be this cold,* Bing thought.

"Who lives here?" he asked, hoping his voice didn't tremble.

"No one," she replied. "It will be George's room when he grows older."

"Isn't the family moving to Toronto?"

"Who told you that?" asked Mrs. Moore. When she spun around, her face was tight.

"I heard Mr. Bentley talking to Mrs. Bentley."

"Oh." Her voice softened. "As far as I know, there's no final decision on the matter. And I don't want to hear another word about it. Understand? Now come along!"

She paused at the door and surveyed the portraits along one wall.

"This room used to belong to Mr. Bentley Sr., the father of the young Mr. Bentley you were spying on."

"Where is Mr. Bentley Sr. now?" he asked.

"He passed away last year. It was a terrible tragedy."

*That explains why this house is haunted,* Bing realized.

Mrs. Moore led him downstairs to the basement and showed him his sleeping quarters. A single electric bulb shed light over the bed and table. The walls weren't finished, and the rows of beams resembled a huge wooden rib cage. In China, no one slept below ground level because people thought the damp air caused stiffness in the fingers and joints.

*Sleeping underground is the same as lying in a grave,* Bing thought.

"There's a storeroom down here too," the housekeeper announced. She led Bing through a door and flicked a switch. Against one wall stood tins of paint. Enough furniture to fill an entire house was stacked there: chairs lying upside down on one another, a table covered by large sheets, a sideboard holding dishes and two bed-frames.

"Come over here," called Mrs. Moore, and Bing made his way toward her.

A sudden noise startled them, and they both spun around. A rocking chair swayed back and forth. Its curved runners scraped the concrete floor.

"Oh, dear boy, you scared me, setting that chair a-rocking."

"I didn't touch it," protested Bing.

He was sure he hadn't brushed against it.

Mrs. Moore went over and stopped the chair, then quickly headed for the door.

"Come along, it's time to put lunch on the table."

Bing kept his distance from the rocker as he followed her upstairs.

When lunch was ready, Bing went to summon Mrs. Bentley to eat. He climbed the rear staircase with care, trying not to make too much noise. Suddenly he heard a loud cough that sounded as deep as Uncle Yung's early morning hacking.

*Who could it be?* Bing wondered. *There are no men in the house now.*

When Bing passed Mr. Bentley Sr.'s room, he pressed his ear to the door. The coughing abruptly stopped. He lightly touched the doorknob, and it felt icy cold.

*It must be a ghost,* he thought, gripping Fortuneteller's stone.

As he backed away, the door in front of him opened, and Mrs. Bentley stood there, coughing into a handkerchief. She was thin and pale, with a freckled face and light-red hair. Her dress, bright green with red ribbons near the neck, seemed too big and made her look almost like a young girl.

"Lunch is served, Ma'am," Bing said, slightly dipping his shoulders.

"You must be the new houseboy. What's your name?"

"Bing."

"Very good, Bing. It's terribly dusty in this room. I'll ask Mrs. Moore to send you back up after lunch. It needs a thorough cleaning."

Bing followed Mrs. Bentley down the stairs and into the dining room, where Mrs. Moore had set out ham and potato salad for Mrs. Bentley's lunch. Bing watched as Mrs. Bentley moved the food from one side of her plate to the other without eating.

"Shall I butter a slice of bread for you?" Mrs. Moore asked.

Mrs. Bentley shook her head.

"Would you prefer to eat something else?" Mrs. Moore asked.

"No thank you. I'm fine."

Mrs. Bentley looked like a ghost to Bing. Her lips were stretched thin and colourless, and her faint blue veins shone through her pale, delicate skin. Dark shadows ringed her eyes.

*Has the ghost invaded her body?* Bing wondered.

Mrs. Bentley caught him staring.

"So, have you seen anything strange in this house?" she snapped. "You people are convinced my house is strange. One minute you're here earning good wages, the next minute you're running down the hill with all your belongings."

"No, Ma'am. I haven't seen anything strange," he said politely.

"He speaks very good English, don't you think, Mrs. Moore? He probably goes to the Mission School."

"No, Ma'am," said Bing. "I attend Central School." He noticed a simple silver crucifix hanging from Mrs. Bentley's neck, identical to the one worn by Mrs. Moore.

*Maybe I should get a Christian cross too,* he thought.

Mrs. Bentley looked at him and raised her eyebrows.

"So, you're not scared?"

"I haven't done anything wrong; so I don't need to be afraid."

"The other Chinese boy left without even asking for his wages. Did you know that?"

"No," Bing lied.

"Well, I find that hard to believe. Don't you, Mrs. Moore? And I certainly hope you turn out to be more dependable, Bing!" She punctuated his name by slamming her palm on the table, and all the dishes and cutlery jumped.

Bing quickly scooped up the serving plates and removed them to the kitchen. He fought the urge to run back to Chinatown. If he went home, everyone would think he was a coward.

# Chapter Seven

B ING SHUDDERED AT THE THOUGHT OF CLEANING MR.
BENTLEY SR.'S ROOM. THE CHILL IN THE ROOM MADE HIM
NERVOUS TO BE THERE ALONE.

Mrs. Moore led him up the stairs and gave him his instructions.

"See this?" she said running a white-gloved finger along a picture frame.

He nodded at the smudge of grey on her glove.

"I don't want to see a speck of dirt when you're finished. Understand?"

"Yes, Ma'am."

"And if you break anything, it's deducted from your wages. Understand?"

"Yes, Ma'am."

The moment she left, Bing drew the curtains to let in as much sunlight as possible. A silver mirror frame reflected the rays of the sun in gleaming bands. He recalled Grandmother saying that mirrors could not show a ghost's image, and that was how one could tell if a stranger was a ghost or a human.

He stared into the mirror and frowned.

*Or perhaps Grandmother really said that mirrors could* reveal *ghostly figures when you thought no one else was in the room with you.*

Bing wished he could remember exactly what she had said. Then, he dampened a rag, dragged a stepladder to the wall and began dusting the tops of the picture frames. In one picture, Bulldog held a large silver trophy as a fierce-looking opponent watched enviously. In another, Bulldog wore a tuxedo with a shiny collar and stood beside his bride on their wedding day. Mrs. Bentley had full cheeks and a radiant smile then. Behind them stood a bear of a man with thick sideburns and eyebrows so bushy there seemed to be no break in between his eyes. He held a huge cigar in his hand.

*That must be Mr. Bentley Sr.,* Bing thought.

Another portrait showed a young woman who must have been Bulldog's mother. She wore a wide, full dress that fanned out in a circle around her hips. Behind her stood two young girls and a boy in a sailor's cap.

*That must be Bulldog as a boy,* Bing thought.

Mr. Bentley Sr. appeared in several formal group portraits labelled *Chamber of Commerce, Board of Trade,* and *The Inaugural Board Meeting of Vancouver Hospital, 1891.* In another photo, he stood surrounded by a group of men in overalls and caps standing under a big sign that read *Bentley Sawmill Company, Ltd., established 1880.*

Bing started to move the ladder but stopped suddenly. He smelled cigar smoke, as strong and pungent as the fumes Lee Dat had exhaled earlier.

*But the ashtrays are all empty,* Bing thought, as the hairs on the back of his neck bristled. *There must be a ghost in this room!*

Terrified, he gripped Fortuneteller's stone and ran down to the kitchen.

"What? Are you finished dusting already?" Mrs. Moore asked.

Bing opened his mouth, but no words came out. What could he say? That a ghost was smoking cigars in that room? That Yawn-mouth had been right to run away from this house?

"Never mind the dusting for now. Go to the store and get me a dozen eggs," Mrs. Moore said.

Bing swallowed gratefully as he headed out the back door. On the road leading downhill, he was sorely tempted to go all the way back to Chinatown; but the thought of Ba and Uncle Won's drivers laughing at his expense stopped him.

*If only Bulldog hadn't gone out of town,* Bing thought. *He would know what to do.*

He passed a mansion with a tall bell turret that could be seen all the way from Chinatown. A streetcar rumbled by. Two men in a clearing chopped at a tree while yoked oxen waited patiently to pull out the stump. Across the street was a tenement block, built as if great boxes had been stacked one atop the other to meet the slope of the hill. He could see three men dash out of a door, pull up their suspenders and hurry down the hill toward False Creek and the sawmills.

The store sign read *O'Brien and Sons,* in fancy letters on a false front billboard. A small bell jangled overhead as Bing went in. The air was rich and warm with the aroma of coffee. Shelves filled with string-tied packages and thick glass jars surrounded an island of barrels in the centre of the store. A chubby woman tottered out from the back of the shop and wiped her hands on her apron. She crooked her neck and squinted at Bing.

"My Lord, child, where did *you* come from?"

"I work for the Bentleys, Ma'am," Bing answered, straightening his shoulders to look taller. "Mrs. Moore sent me."

The woman froze. Then her hand darted from one shoulder to the other, making the sign of the cross.

"Please, Ma'am," Bing said. "I just need a dozen eggs."

The shopkeeper counted eggs from a metal basket into a paper bag.

"Ten cents," she demanded.

Bing gave her the money and took the bag.

Outside, he noticed a large handbill tacked to the door of the tenement block.

*What if one of the mills wants to hire workers? Maybe I could change jobs and get away from the Bentley house!*

When Bing crossed the road to look more closely at the notice, two men lurched out from behind the tenement building.

"What's in the bag, boy? Snack for me?"

Stubble covered the man's face. Bloodshot eyes suggested he was drunk. His red-checked shirt hung stiff, caked with something brown. He smelled like garbage.

"Hey, Charlie," he called to his friend. "You hungry?"

"Them Chinks eat cats," cackled Charlie. "You don't want to see what's in that bag."

They chortled, and Bing darted aside to get around them. But Red Checks stepped in front of him, blocking his way. When Bing tried to step around him, Red Checks blocked him again.

"Is my buddy right? You got kittens in that bag?"

Bing wanted to fling the eggs into his face, but he spun around and ran back across the street to the store.

*No point going in there,* he thought.

He headed up the hill at the back of the store and prayed that the men wouldn't follow him; but if they did, he would hurl the eggs at them. The slope was thick with underbrush, and the only easy way to get back to the Bentleys was to turn around. But that meant confronting Red Checks again.

There was no choice but to head into the bushes and tramp through the forest. He ducked under low-hanging branches, climbed over rotting logs and almost slipped into a swamp. The air was thick with buzzing insects.

*If only I'd been trained in the martial arts!* he thought.

Back at the house, Mrs. Moore peered into the bag of eggs in order to count them and inspect for damage.

Then she pointed to a trail of dirt between the kitchen door and the ice chest.

"What a mess you've made! And I thought you finished cleaning Mr. Bentley Sr.'s room. You left the job half done, and you'll have to finish it tomorrow! Now, go scrub yourself up and then clean up this mess!"

While Bing swept up, he heard a piano and a solemn voice singing hymns. Now that the house was filled with songs praising the Christian God's glory, he felt a little safer.

"Bing, come meet Master George. Come see my baby," Mrs. Bentley called from the parlour.

She cradled the infant in her arms. The wisps of fine hair on his head glowed a deep orange. George's blue eyes were wide open, and he stared at Bing without blinking.

"How old is he?" Bing asked, patting George's tiny hand.

"Three months."

"He looks happy," said Bing, surprised at how friendly Mrs. Bentley could be.

"Oh, he's a very cheerful baby. He's never been sick or given me a moment's care."

That night, Bing placed his new clothes at the foot of his bed. He wanted to be able to jump into them at the slightest sign of a ghost. He left the electric light on and slid under the blanket. His hands were cold when he pressed them together to recite the Lord's Prayer. Baby George was crying upstairs. Bing sniffed the air.

*At least there's no smell of cigar smoke,* he thought.

He put Fortuneteller's stone, a candle and a small box of matches under his pillow. Touching these now, he felt a sense of safety. Back in China, Mother and Grandmother had often sat by his bed reciting ancient rhymes and tales to lull him to sleep. Bing pulled the blanket close and recalled one of those stories where the ghost had been defeated:

*Long ago, a judge was appointed to a court in a faraway city; so he moved there and bought a mansion. The price was low because the house was haunted. But he thought no ghost would dare bother a judge. So he moved in.*

*On the first night, he awoke and saw a man standing by the window, looking outside.*

*"Who are you?" he called out.*

*"A ghost," came the reply.*

*The judge thought quickly and declared, "I am a ghost too. What do you want?"*

*"This was my house, and the garden I built is beautiful under a full moon."*

*The judge went outside to look at the walled garden. The ghost followed him outside. There were ancient trees, rock sculptures and a pool with a bridge arching over a small stream. The moon set everything aglow. The summer night was very warm.*

*"Let's go down and sit in the moonlight," the judge said, smiling at the ghost.*

*"Why do your feet make so much noise?" the ghost asked.*

*"I died just a few days ago, so I haven't learned to walk like you."*

*They sat by the pool and listened to the rustle of a willow tree.*

*The ghost looked into the water and asked, "Why do you still cast a reflection?"*

*"I am a new ghost. My physical soul is still present. Is it true that ghosts are afraid of water?"*

*"Yes, because water is heavier than air. I wish I could cool myself in this water."*

*"Go on," urged the judge. "Take a dip. Nothing will happen."*

*So the ghost slid into the water and swam back and forth. As it glided by the judge, he scooped it up in a bucketful of water. Then the judge hurried out to the road and threw the water into a ditch.*

*The ghost never came back again, and the judge lived a long and prosperous life.*

The next thing Bing knew, someone was banging on his door, calling his name. The windows above his head showed daylight. He leapt out of bed.

*I survived the night,* he rejoiced. *There's nothing to fear! The ghost has no cause to harm me. If I mind my own business, it will leave me alone. But can living in a haunted house that scares even the local shopkeepers be this easy?* he wondered.

After breakfast, Bing summoned up the courage to go finish the job in Mr. Bentley Sr.'s room. He entered cautiously and took a deep breath. He smelled leather, faint perfumes and a pouch of dried lavender left atop the chest of drawers. But no cigar smoke.

Bing sagged with relief and clutched Fortuneteller's stone.

*It still works!* he surmised.

# Chapter Eight

BING TUGGED ON HIS OLD CLOTHES AND HEADED FOR CHINATOWN. HE HELD HIS FIRST WEEK'S PAY IN HIS HAND WITH A DEEP SENSE OF PRIDE. HE HAD LASTED A WHOLE WEEK IN A HOUSE HE KNEW WAS HAUNTED.

Because streetcars didn't run on Sundays, he set out on foot, running down Fairview Hill and heading north across the Cambie Bridge. The sun cast a soft glow over rowboats swaying gently on the water. To the west, the sawmills were silent; their blades were idle today and no smoke darkened the sky.

Bing imagined taking centre stage at Uncle Won's store to describe the ghostly happenings at the Bentley house. The drivers' mouths would fall open on hearing that Yawn-mouth Yuen's story was true. Ba would have to give Bing respect and also admit to being wrong about ghosts. Ba would never be able to call him a coward again!

Close to Chinatown, the squawk of cooped chickens rose above the hubbub of crowded streets. Sunday was the busiest shopping day. Outside the Methodist Mission, Christians gathered around a portable organ and sang hymns. On an adjacent corner, two lottery ticket sellers called out for customers. A cobbler offered to repair shoes, his toolbox open on the sidewalk. Men hurried toward restaurants and gambling halls. Every seat was taken at the barbershop. Woong-Woong, the three-legged stray dog, waited for leftovers at the Apricot Blossom restaurant. A waiter dashed out with a tray of covered bowls, filled with hot rice porridge.

Bing wanted to tell James how Fortuneteller's stone had saved him from the Bentley ghost. But Bing's first stop had to be Ba's room or else he'd be accused of being disrespectful.

Ba was in bed, covered by a mountain of heavy blankets. A knitted hat was pulled down to his brow, and a terrible wheezing came from his half-open mouth. Stifled by the stale air, Bing flung open the window. A bowl with aromatic oils sat atop the box that served as a bedside table. Inside the box was a bucket reeking of vomit and urine.

Ba was pale, and thick stubble shadowed his face. Suddenly, he jerked up and started coughing violently. He threw his blankets aside as spasms shook his body. Bing looked away when Ba reached for the bucket and retched into it. Bing had never seen his father so sick.

"Go get me some water," ordered Ba.

Bing ran to the kitchen and filled a glass jar from the pot of cool, boiled water.

Back upstairs Ba was sitting up, tying his bootlaces. He grabbed the glass jar and drank greedily, water streaming down his chin and throat. He wiped his mouth with a sleeve and then turned to Bing with feverish eyes.

"I've been waiting for you. We're going out."

"You're not well. You should stay in bed."

"You're a doctor?" snapped his father. "You think I'm dying?"

Bing clamped his mouth shut as Ba staggered down the stairs. They took the back door into the courtyard, and Bing helped Ba hitch Red Hare to one of the wagons. Then Ba fetched shovels and a bulging burlap sack from the storage shed.

*Bones!* Bing thought. *Oh no!*

Ba heaved the sack onto the wagon and jumped aboard, seizing the reins. Reluctantly, Bing joined him, arms crossed over his chest.

As Ba whipped Red Hare into a gallop, dust swirled from his hooves. Gravel spat out from wheels spinning so fast that their spokes blurred.

They shot past people dressed in their Sunday best, returning from prayer services. A white man shook his fist and cursed them for driving so fast, but Ba paid no attention. The shovels rattling in the back suggested one destination to Bing—the graveyard. Shouting like a drunken madman, Ba whipped the horse until the speeding wagon seemed about to skid and overturn. Bing glanced at Ba nervously.

*Has the ghost of the bones invaded his body?* Bing wondered.

Bing reached for Fortuneteller's stone but couldn't find it. In his rush to leave the Bentley house, he must have left it in his new trousers.

When they reached the cemetery, Ba yelled, "Bring the shovels!" and headed for the Chinese section.

He paced anxiously around Shum's grave, muttering to himself and casting nervous glances at the soil. Bing dropped the shovels on the ground and looked around. Not far from them, groups of visitors stood with heads quietly bowed over newly filled graves. Mounds of freshly turned soil revealed where Ba had removed other bones before falling sick.

"Where are the shovels?" demanded Ba.

"By the head of the grave."

"Where?"

"Right there," said Bing, pointing to a spot near where Ba stood.

"Where?" Ba snarled with impatience.

Bing glanced up and down the rows of graves, but the shovels were gone.

"I put them right there," Bing declared.

He shook his head and thought, *No one could have sneaked up and stolen them! I was standing right there!*

He swallowed hard and inched away from Shum's grave.

"A thief followed us," Ba said accusingly. "You should have been watching closely."

He darted off and returned with two short wooden planks. His eyes glinted, hot with fever. "We'll use these to dig," he shouted. Then he thrust the plank into the ground, pressed down and squatted to lift the soil.

"Waiting to die?" he growled at Bing. "Get over here. Get to work!"

The two of them crouched and dug, side by side. The work went slowly, because the planks were awkward to use. Every now and then Ba exploded in a coughing fit that doubled him over. After the coughing subsided, the only sounds Bing heard were the scrape of wood against rock and the soft thud of earth landing on grass. Dirt seeped into Bing's boots and between his toes.

Soon they had to jump into the open grave to continue their work. Grit blew into Bing's eyes, and tears made him squint. The heavy board kept slipping from his grip. His hands grew sweaty, new blisters were forming and his back began to ache. Every now and then, he stopped to pick out splinters from his fingers. Finally, when the hole was deep enough, Ba dropped his plank and boosted Bing out of the pit.

"Go get the bones," Ba said.

When Bing came back with the sack of bones, he saw his father standing at the bottom of the pit, staring at the ground.

*I wonder if he's found the missing skull?* he thought.

Bing set down the bulging sack and asked timidly, "Have you found anything there?"

Ba didn't answer. Instead, Bing saw his father quickly burrow down and scoop out the loose earth with his bare hands. Then Ba began to tug feverishly at something. Whatever it was, it refused to budge. Ba grunted and cursed loudly. Finally, he managed to dislodge two long objects.

*It's the missing shovels!* Bing thought. *Shum's ghost is toying with us! It's angry! Something horrible will happen!*

As Ba heaved the missing shovels onto the grass beside the pit, Bing turned and ran.

He hid behind Red Hare and tried to stop himself from shaking. He knew he should help Ba out of the crumbling grave, but fear paralyzed him.

From a safe distance, Bing watched his father clamber out of the open grave, lift the white bundle of bones out of the sack and carefully place it on the ground next to the grave. Then Ba opened the bundle. Bing gulped and squeezed his eyes shut, afraid to see what might happen next.

"Nothing to fear, Little One!" Ba shouted, challenging him.

Bing opened his eyes a crack and watched his father lay out the skeleton: the tall leg bones beside the tiny bones of the feet, the long arm bones beside the many shards that formed the hands. Nimbly, Ba jumped from side to side, sliding bones into their correct places like a life-size jigsaw puzzle. After he made sure all the bones were there, he carefully piled them one atop another, leg bones crossed at the bottom, the hips in the middle and the ribs and arms near the top. Then, he gathered up the cloth tightly and knotted it firmly before lowering the bundle into the grave.

"Help me cover up the bones," Ba said, picking up one of the newly recovered shovels. "It won't take long now that we've got our shovels back."

Bing shook his head obstinately and climbed onto the wagon.

*How could Ba bear to touch a shovel that had just been stolen by a powerful spirit?*

Ba quickly shovelled dirt back into the grave. When the ground was level again, he retrieved the wooden marker and planted it firmly. Then he brought the shovels over and flung them into the wagon. Bing jumped at the clatter they made.

"Don't say a word about this to anyone, understand?" said Ba.


As soon as the wagon reached Uncle Won's courtyard, Bing jumped off and dashed through the store onto the street.

"Come back here!" Ba shouted.

Bing paid no attention. He ran past the church, past the satisfied diners emerging from restaurants and past the letter writer's table in front of the Lun Chong general store.

Bing burst into Uncle Jong's store. It was silent except for the tick-tock of the grandfather clock. He passed the sewing machines smelling of lubricating oil. At the partition that separated the factory from the living quarters, there was an oilcloth-covered table with teacups soaking in a pan of water, a stack of recent newspapers and assorted jars of ointment.

"Anyone home?" Bing called out.

"Where'd you come from?" asked James, emerging from the back of the shop. "You're dirty as a pig."

"Shum's ghost is chasing me!" Bing felt the fine hairs on the back of his neck suddenly stand up. "Ba made me help him rebury Shum's bones."

"Sounds like nonsense."

"It's true!"

"And if I don't think so?"

"Here, see how cold my hands are."

James sat down, ignoring him. "Where's the stone from Fortuneteller?"

"In my other trousers back at the Bentley house."

"Did you see any ghosts there too?"

"Of course!" said Bing. "Good thing Fortuneteller gave me that stone."

"You sure you're not imagining things?"

"Why would I make that up?"

"So there is a ghost up there?"

Bing nodded.

"Then you may need this." James went to the counter, rummaged in a drawer and tossed Bing a cross on a chain.

Bing turned it over and saw a pair of tiny doves etched into the centre.

"You shouldn't be working at that house," James continued. "Did you tell your father about the ghost?"

"What for? He doesn't believe in ghosts. It was Mother and Grandmother who told me stories about ghosts."

"Yes, those stories are about people who died unhappily, before they had time to get married or have a child. Or they were killed during a robbery or drowned in a boat accident. They haven't lived their full lives, and they wander about the earth as ghosts seeking revenge or looking for another chance at life. But your family spirits can protect you from them."

"Then Ba should be burning offerings to protect us from Shum's ghost, don't you think?"

"Yes."

James went to the counter and returned with thin sheets of rice paper with tiny holes punched in them. "Here's some ghost money. Maybe you can burn it and that will appease Shum's ghost."

Bing took the ghost money and put it in his pocket along with the cross.

*You can never have too much protection,* Bing thought.

"Where is Uncle Jong?" Bing asked.

"There's a big meeting at the Council. They're starting up a Chinatown patrol to protect us. Some guards will even be carrying guns."

"Isn't that the job of the police?"

"The police are like everybody else. They think that too many Chinese live here. They want to drive the Chinese out of town. They did it twenty years ago; now they want to do it again."

"Do you think that the patrol will be able to protect me outside of Chinatown? I ran into two men in Fairview who taunted me," he said.

"Did you fight?"

"Couldn't. I was carrying a dozen eggs back to the mansion."

"Carry a cudgel with you next time. You had better learn to protect yourself from the whites. The patrol won't be able to protect you outside of Chinatown. Hey, hasn't your boss taught you boxing yet?"

"No."

"I told you he wouldn't."

"He's gone on a tour, fighting in a whole bunch of cities."

"Bet you he won't teach you anything."

"Bet you he will. He'll remember me from the class."

"Let's put money on this."

"You're on!"

"How much?"

"Ten cents."

"Done!"

# Chapter Nine

BETTER TO TRAVEL WHEN IT'S STILL LIGHT, BING THOUGHT AS HE TRUDGED OVER THE CAMBIE BRIDGE ON HIS WAY BACK TO THE BENTLEY HOUSE.

*Shum's ghost might be lurking in the shadows looking for his head. Ba shouldn't be going around unearthing the bones of strangers. The spirits of those people may not want their bones removed. Shum was perfectly happy down in his little hole. Being dug up and taken back into the world of the living made him angry.*

*And what exactly has upset Mr. Bentley Sr.'s ghost?* Bing wondered, as he entered the long driveway leading up to the mansion.

What he saw as he approached the house filled him with excitement. A new motorcar was parked at the side entrance. In Chinatown, only the rich merchant Chang Toy owned such a vehicle. It stayed padlocked behind sturdy doors when not on the road, so nobody could go near it.

Bing approached the motorcar and ran his hand over the still warm bonnet. There were deep wheel-wells, high-mounted lamps, a padded steering wheel and a trunk strapped to the running board.

*Maybe this sleek machine has been delivered for Bulldog, and I'll be assigned to clean it! Maybe I could even make a quick trip to Chinatown and back!*

He rushed into the house, and there was a note waiting for him on the kitchen table with a list of all the chores for the coming week:

PREPARE BREAKFAST

EMPTY THE CHAMBER POT IN THE MAIN BEDROOM

REPLENISH THE WATER AND TOWELS ON THE WASHSTAND

WASH THE BABY'S CLOTHES AND DIAPERS

WAX AND BUFF TABLETOPS

SWEEP FLOORS AND STAIRS

BEAT CARPETS

PEEL POTATOES FOR EVENING MEAL

SCRUB POTS

POLISH SILVERWARE

REMOVE ASHES FROM THE CATCH-PAN UNDER THE STOVE
GRIND THE MEAT
CHOP WOOD
WATER THE GARDEN

Bing heard Mrs. Bentley's voice coming from the conservatory. "Gerald, how much longer before this house will be sold?"

"Impossible to say. My motto is *Never make promises that can't be kept.*"

"Give me a general idea. I need to start packing soon."

"It's only been two weeks. Don't forget that it's difficult selling houses in the summer. Once autumn arrives, people will get serious about real estate. Right now everyone is on holiday. Everyone wants to enjoy the good weather before the rain starts."

"I saw Philip Ross in church the other day. He just sold three houses."

"Hah!" hooted Gerald. "He's selling flimsy shacks to factory workers on the East Side. Your house is different. Why, this is a mansion!"

"Philip Ross claims he can sell this place in a week."

"He's lying. Did he ask you to lower the price?"

She didn't answer, and the agent went on quickly. "See what I mean? If you let me reduce the price, I could sell this place in a flash."

Then his tone softened. "Besides, I have to counter that gossip. There's a rumour that this house is haunted, you know."

"That's all it is. Gossip and dirty lies."

"But why didn't the roofer fix your leak? I heard one man came out but jumped off his ladder in a panic."

"I don't know. I wasn't here."

The two fell silent for a moment before the agent spoke again. "I'm your husband's best friend, and I knew your father-in-law well. I promise you I'll get the right price for this house."

Mrs. Moore suddenly stepped up behind Bing.

"My, you're back early, Bing," she remarked, pulling off her gloves.

"The real estate agent is here," he whispered.

Mrs. Moore's lips tightened. "Good luck to him," she muttered.

"How long before Mr. Bentley comes home?" asked Bing.

"Not soon enough to stop this nonsense," she sighed, donning an apron.

"I saw your list. Where should I start?"

"Have you had your supper?"

"I'm not hungry, thank you."

"Then go to your room. You can help me with breakfast in the morning."

In his room, Bing reached for his good pair of pants and fished out Fortuneteller's stone. Then he put it under his pillow along with the cross, undressed and went to bed.

He was sound asleep when a persistent thumping woke him. His eyes flicked open. Someone was banging on the front door. Far above, baby George began to wail. Bing reached for Fortuneteller's stone and turned on the light. He heard footsteps on the main stairs.

"Coming! I'm coming. Just a minute!" Mrs. Moore called out hoarsely.

*It must be a Bentley relative,* Bing thought. He prayed he wouldn't have to go upstairs to prepare the guestroom at this hour.

"Who's out there? Show yourself, you hear me?" Mrs. Moore called out. "You don't frighten me one bit. Don't you know that? Come here this instant so I can see you."

*It must be the ghost!* Bing thought. He pulled the covers up over his head.

As he heard Mrs. Moore double lock the door, he fumbled underneath his pillow for James' cross and tightly clutched it in his other hand.

Baby George's crying turned to wails.

*If only Bulldog were here. He'd be able to protect us all from the ghost.*

Suddenly the pounding at the front door started up again. Bing tightened his grip on the stone and the cross as the very walls of the house started to shake.

"Who's there?" Mrs. Moore shouted fearfully. "Go away and don't bother us. Do you hear me? I said, leave us alone! This is the house of honest people."

Bing bolted upright in bed.

*This must have been what sent Yawn-mouth Yuen fleeing for his life.*

He put the cross around his neck and recited Fortuneteller's chant until he fell asleep, exhausted.

*He who does only right,*
*Will never ever know fright.*
*Not even from rapping at the door,*
*At three in the morning or at four.*

The next morning, Bing was relieved to hear Mrs. Moore bustling in the kitchen. She dropped coal and wood into the stove and filled the kettle with water. He pocketed the stone and the cross and went up to start his morning chores. But the kitchen was filled with smoke. He flailed at the thick grey clouds, looking for Mrs. Moore.

"Fire!" he shouted, rushing to the sink for water.

But the housekeeper shushed him. "Quiet! Nothing's wrong."

Bing covered his nose with his hand and saw smoke spewing from every crack and opening in the stove. Mrs. Moore stuck a stool against the back door to keep it open.

She climbed onto a chair to reach the damper in the chimney behind the stove. The knob squeaked, and suddenly the fire in the stove crackled and resumed burning.

"How did the damper get closed?" asked Bing.

"I don't know. And don't tell anyone! Did you fiddle with the damper?"

"No, Ma'am," Bing gulped.

"Open all the windows, quick. We need to clear out this smoke before Mrs. Bentley comes down."

Baby George was wailing again.

"I'd better go tend to the baby. You start the breakfast," Mrs. Moore said.

Once the kitchen was clear of smoke, Bing set water to boil and stirred in porridge oats. From the ice chest, he took out butter to let it soften. He made toast by setting a metal rack of bread over the flames.

*The ghost must have shut the damper on the chimney pipe!* he thought. *Maybe it was angry because Mrs. Moore wouldn't open the door last night.*

"Mrs. Bentley is upset because she couldn't sleep last night," Mrs. Moore said under her breath as she returned. "And now little George won't let her rest. I offered to take the baby, but she insists the child only wants her. A baby knows when its mother is upset. He'll cry all morning, mark my words."

"Who was at the door last night?" asked Bing as he removed the toast.

"Who knows? Probably drunken workers from the sawmills."

Bing heard the crunch of wooden wheels on the driveway. The noise grew louder as a wagon drew closer. A horse snorted louder and louder, whinnying as the driver tried to coax it up to the house. Bing ran out to see if he could help.

A speckled grey mare flailed in a frenzy, hooves thrashing from side to side. Its ears were pressed back tight against its head, and the terrified whites of its eyes glared at the mansion.

"Bessie, Bessie," shouted the driver. "Down, girl, down."

The horse reared, then shook her mane and veered off, yanking the reins from the driver. The wagon rumbled behind her in a storm of dust.

"Damn!" The driver slammed his cap onto the ground.

Mrs. Moore rushed to the gate, shading her eyes against the sun.

"Bing," she called. "Go fetch the cart from the shed. You can follow Mr. Crew to the next house and bring back the ice. His horse and wagon will be there, waiting for him."

She spoke so calmly that Bing suspected this had happened before.

Mr. Crew waited with Bessie at the next house. He used steel tongs to heave a block of ice onto Bing's cart. He covered the ice with gunnysacks and grabbed the cart's handle.

"I get paid to deliver ice directly into the ice chest. A wee runt like you can't move this!"

They headed back together.

"What happened to your horse?" asked Bing.

"My Bessie has run this route for six years and never had no trouble. But three weeks ago, every time we get near that house Bessie has a fit. Where's that boy Yuen? Didn't he stay to help pack up the house for the big move?"

"He quit. And the house hasn't sold yet."

Mr. Crew wiped sweat from his neck. "It's going to take a while, if you ask me. There are strange happenings here. Everyone knows that." He peered at Bing. "What about you? Have you seen anything strange goin' on?"

Bing shrugged his shoulders. "Do you know how Mr. Bentley Sr. died?"

"Fell off a ladder. He was fixing the roof, I heard. Broke his neck and that was the end of him."

*An accident!* Bing felt relieved. *At least Mr. Bentley wasn't murdered,* he thought.

"By the way, little fella, if you get sent to buy things at the O'Brien store, watch out for Charlie and his friend the big ape. You can smell them a block away, 'cause they never wash. If they're not too drunk to stand up, they're always makin' trouble on the streets. They grabbed a houseboy from another house and beat him so badly he went to hospital."

"The two from the big rooming house?"

"Have you run into them already?" Mr. Crew turned to face Bing. "They don't have jobs. Never had one. Never will. You'd best stay out of their way."

*I'd like to fight them to the death,* thought Bing.

They went through the gate, and the iceman shook his head. "Watch out for yourself. You're a long way from home."

# Chapter Ten

BING WATCHED FROM THE KITCHEN AS MRS. MOORE SERVED MRS. BENTLEY BREAKFAST. THERE WERE BLACK SMUDGES BENEATH MRS. BENTLEY'S EYES, AND HER HAIR HUNG IN A DULL TANGLE, UNCOMBED AND UNBRUSHED. THE BABY WAS WAILING UPSTAIRS, BUT THE TWO WOMEN IGNORED HIM.

"After breakfast, I want you to get Mr. Rogers on the telephone for me," Mrs. Bentley said to her housekeeper, as Mrs. Moore brought in the poached eggs. "I want to tell him to reduce the price of the house. After last night's racket, I want to leave for Toronto as soon as possible."

"Yes, Ma'am," she frowned.

Bing entered the dining room and poured tea into Mrs. Bentley's gold-rimmed teacup.

"This tea is far too strong," she said.

"I'll add some hot water, Ma'am."

Bing took the teapot away.

"Go fetch George," she ordered Mrs. Moore. "And do something about his wailing. He's been crying all night, and nothing seems to soothe him."

"Maybe it's time to call the doctor," Mrs. Moore said, turning to go upstairs.

Bing diluted the tea and returned to the dining room, just as Mrs. Moore came back down with George. His tiny fists hammered the air as he wriggled and howled.

"These eggs are cold," scowled Mrs. Bentley. "Bring me some freshly poached eggs instead."

Mrs. Moore deftly handed the infant to Bing and went into the kitchen.

George immediately stopped crying. Bing rocked him, and the baby gurgled and cooed.

"Ah, finally the rascal is settling down!" Mrs. Bentley burst out happily. "Have you taken care of many babies?"

"No, Ma'am."

Bing had never held a baby. Back home in China, young girls and older sisters minded the infants, while the few families in Chinatown who had babies also had maidservants and nurses. One of George's little hands tugged at Bing's sleeve.

"Do you know magic spells then?"

Bing shook his head.

"Little George misses his father. He'll sleep much better once Robert returns," Mrs. Bentley said.

"Yes, Ma'am. When will he be back?"

Mrs. Bentley acted as if she hadn't heard. Bing gently swung Little George to and fro, and the baby gurgled contentedly.

Mrs. Moore returned with a fresh batch of eggs and served Mrs. Bentley. Then the housekeeper took the baby from Bing.

"Go do your morning chores now," she ordered.

Bing hurried up the servant's staircase to Mrs. Bentley's bedroom, where he made the bed and tidied up the room. Then he removed the chamber pot and the dirty diapers. He then cleaned up the water closet and refreshed the towels.

Bing's next chore was to dust the books in the parlour. The leather-bound volumes had titles embossed in gold along the spines: hymn books, prayer books, biographies of Queen Victoria, books of poetry, a well-thumbed *Manual for Mothers* and several books on etiquette. He also discovered *Health Exercises*, *Home Gymnastics without Appliances* and *The National Amateur Boxing Guide*.

*Maybe this is how Bulldog learned to box*, Bing thought. *Maybe this is an illustrated manual that teaches boxing.*

Next to *The National Amateur Boxing Guide* was a book called *The Boxers*. Bing pulled that out as well and flipped through the pages. There were long chapters, illustrated with drawings of fighters. Before he could examine it more closely, Mrs. Bentley interrupted him.

"What do you think you're doing?"

"Nothing, Ma'am," said Bing, dropping the book.

"These are our personal books," she said, swooping across the room and picking up the book.

"Why, Bing, what a surprise! Are you a fan of my husband's boxing?"

"Mr. Bentley came to my school and taught our athletics class."

"I've always despised this little book. It's time to get rid of it."

She turned abruptly and headed downstairs to the kitchen. Bing hurried after her and saw her drop the book into the stove.

"Mr. Bentley won't be needing this once we move to Toronto. He'll have a proper position with my father's firm."

She spun around and left the kitchen just as Mrs. Moore entered.

"Well, well, well. What was that all about?" she asked.

"Mrs. Bentley threw one of Mr. Bentley's boxing books into the stove."

"Mrs. Bentley thinks boxing is low-class entertainment, too rough for people of her station, too embarrassing for a well-established family such as hers."

"But Bulldog is the best fighter this city has ever seen."

"Oh, I'm well aware of that, and I'm very proud of him. But Mrs. Bentley thinks boxing is a violent sport and Mr. Bentley might get seriously injured. That's one of the reasons she wants to move to Toronto."

Late that afternoon, Mr. Rogers pulled up the driveway as Bing was mopping the front porch.

"Where is Mrs. Moore?" he asked Bing. "I have clients in the car who want to see the house."

"I'm right here," Mrs. Moore said, rounding the corner. "You promised to give us a day's warning before bringing people to view the house!"

"These people are from Winnipeg. They're going back on tonight's train. And they're the right people for this house."

"But the house isn't ready to be shown. I'm cooking right now!"

"They're eager to buy. They've already fallen in love with the view of the mountains from this hill."

"I have a roast on the stove!"

"As you know, Mrs. Bentley spoke with me on the telephone this morning to say that she's very anxious to sell the house."

"Oh, very well. Just give us a few minutes. Bring your clients into the parlour."

"That Mr. Rogers has some nerve, bringing people here without notice," she grumbled as she headed back to the kitchen with Bing. "I wish Mr. Bentley were here."

"If Mr. Bentley were home maybe the house wouldn't be for sale."

"Yes," she smiled. "Wouldn't that be nice?"

Then they heard a cart coming around to the back door.

"Now who could that be!" exclaimed Mrs. Moore. "The last thing we need is another peddler coming around. Oh, it's Mr. Bates, the egg man."

"Good afternoon, Mrs. Moore," the egg man said.

"Good afternoon, Mr. Bates," Mrs. Moore responded.

Suddenly, a shrill scream pierced the air. The kitchen door burst open and the woman buyer rushed out. As she raced past them, her broad-brimmed hat lifted like a kite and sailed up for a moment before drifting to the ground. But she didn't stop. Her male companion dashed out behind her and scooped up the hat without slowing his pace.

As they ran around to the front of the house, Bing, Mrs. Moore and Mr. Bates, the egg man, followed closely behind. The man opened the motorcar door, pushed the woman inside and slammed the door shut.

Mr. Rogers darted from the house, cranked the motorcar's engine and jumped aboard. As they drove away, Bing glimpsed three faces staring wild-eyed through the windows.

"I'll not be coming here any more," said Mr. Bates turning to Mrs. Moore. "There are too many strange goings on here."

Just then, Mrs. Bentley appeared at the front door, her hands trembling as she pointed toward the parlour. Her eyes stared straight ahead. When Mrs. Moore approached her, Mrs. Bentley sagged into the housekeeper's arms and whimpered like a sick child.

Mrs. Moore gently led Mrs. Bentley back to the parlour and Bing followed behind.

The parlour was a jumble of pillows, cushions and shards of glass. The large mirror over the mantle was a web of dark cracks and shattered glass. Bing reached for Fortuneteller's stone and held it in one hand while grasping James' cross in his other hand.

He wanted to run out of the room, but he wasn't able to move a muscle.

Then, without any warning, the brass spittoon began to roll across the floor in a slow wobble. Picking up speed, it slammed into Bing's leg, and Fortuneteller's stone flew from his hand, falling through the hot-air grate. Bing yelped loudly and bolted down the front hallway and out the front door as fast as his legs could carry him.

# September 1907
# Between Two Worlds

# Chapter Eleven

**B**ING RAN ALL THE WAY TO THE CAMBIE BRIDGE WITHOUT STOPPING. HE WANTED TO GET AS FAR AWAY FROM THE BENTLEY HOUSE AS HE COULD. HE KNEW THAT, WHEN PROVOKED, AN ANGRY GHOST COULD EMPTY VILLAGES AND CRIPPLE STRONG MEN.

*What if the Bentley ghost has invaded my body? What if my life is fading away with every step I take?*

When he reached the Cambie Bridge, Bing dodged through crowds of men who were heading home from work. On the other side of False Creek, he ran west along the waterfront toward the commercial district, instead of into Chinatown.

*If I go home,* Bing thought, *I'll have to face Ba, who'll call me a coward. The drivers around the dinner table will shake their heads and call me a child. Uncle Sing will mutter, 'What's there to be scared of? So there was a ghost. It didn't bite you, did it?'*

He crossed railway tracks where a slow-moving locomotive, clanging an iron bell in warning, tugged a line of flat cars. He sprinted past heavily loaded wagons, secured with nets, that horses strained to pull. Too exhausted to go any further, Bing leaned against the railing by the water's edge. Sweat trickled down his face. The vast harbour stretched out in front of him. Water lapped up against the wooden pilings as the tide came in. The horn of a passing steamship sent Bing into a daydream.

*I should go back to China,* he thought, *where I belong. I could stow away aboard a ship. The Chinese sailors will give me leftover food so I won't starve. I'll even mop the decks. After the boat docks, I'll find a way to our village, and Grandmother will open her arms and welcome me home.*

"Hey, Bing-bong, what's garbage like you doing here? This is a respectable place," Freddie Cox said as he slapped him on the back.

Bing turned around and saw Freddie with two other boys he did not recognize.

"None of your business," Bing replied, turning his back to them.

"Hey, Ding-dong, did you come here for a swim?" Freddie grabbed his shoulder.

Bing pulled away, but the boys circled him and pushed him toward the edge of the dock. "I think you're right," one said. "He looks awful dirty. He needs a bath!"

"Let me go!" Bing shouted, trying to free himself.

"Don't you want to go swimming?" insisted Freddie, reaching for Bing's legs.

"No! Let me go!" Bing shouted as his feet were swept out from under him.

Just as the three boys lifted Bing over the edge of the railing, a man's voice boomed out, "Hey, stop what you do!"

Bing twisted free. It was Dent-head Fong, on a wagon behind Red Hare. Bing ran over and clambered aboard.

"Coward! Baby! Stinker!" the bullies jeered and hooted.

"What are you doing here, Little One?" Dent-head Fong asked, as the wagon pulled away. "Shouldn't you be at work?"

Bing didn't answer.

*If only Bulldog had given me a few lessons,* he thought. *Then I could have fought them off all by myself!*

Without uttering another word, Dent-head drove the wagon back to Uncle Won's store.

Bing expected to smell dinner coming out of the kitchen and to hear men shouting stories about the day's deliveries.

Instead, he saw drivers hammering nails and sawing long beams of fresh lumber. Even Uncle Won and Uncle Sing were helping out. James was in the courtyard as well, dragging planks into the alley where the men were building a fence.

"What's going on?" Bing asked.

"We're building a fence," replied James. "What are you doing here?"

"The housekeeper sent me over to fetch something from the market," Bing lied.

"In Chinatown?" James snorted. "Come here and give us a hand."

Bing helped James carry several planks to the alley.

"Why are we building a fence?" Bing asked.

"This morning the drivers came down and found one of the horses dead."

"Dead! Which one?"

"The grey-speckled one. Uncle Won thinks a white man poisoned it."

Bing's stomach tightened. *At least Red Hare is safe,* he thought.

"The only way to protect the other horses," James said, "is to seal off the courtyard. There's going to be big trouble. Chinatown will explode like a keg of gunpowder. You better see your father. He's very sick. Your Uncle Won thinks it's something serious."

"What?"

"Fortuneteller went to see your father today, but Ba won't tell anyone what he said. Go ask him."

As he entered Ba's room, Bing saw Broken-leg kick his father, who was lying crumpled on the floor.

"Leave my father alone! He's sick!" Bing shouted.

"He's faking," retorted Broken-leg. "He's too lazy to work, too lazy to repay his debts. Useless people like him deserve to die!"

Broken-leg kicked Ba again, and he rolled away, moaning in agony.

"They say blood can't be squeezed from a stone," Broken-leg said, pressing his boot into Ba's face. "But it's not the same for a man, is it?"

"Stop!" Bing pleaded.

"I can't go back to my boss without some money."

"No money here," Ba muttered weakly.

"Didn't you hear me the first time? I can't leave without a payment."

"I'll pay," Ba whimpered. "I promise. Just give me time."

"You're out of time. Don't gamble if you don't have the money to pay up."

"I work!" shouted Bing. "I can pay you!"

"How?"

"I'm a houseboy in Fairview. I earn five dollars a week. You can have it all."

"You're lying."

"Go ask Lee Dat."

"If you're lying, I'll beat the life out of you, Little One." And with that, Broken-Leg strode out.

Bing helped his father get back into bed.

"I don't need your money," Ba said. "I can take care of myself."

"Hah! You can't even stand up by yourself. What did Fortuneteller say?"

"Nothing."

"You're lying. I'll go ask him myself."

"You don't know where to go."

"Who says? Just watch me."

"Stay out of my affairs! Do you hear me? Stay out of my affairs."

"It's too late for that!"

Bing hurried over to Fortuneteller's room in the Kwong Yuen store. His door was slightly ajar, so Bing pushed it open and walked in. The room reeked of incense. The afternoon light revealed a map of the world on the wall. Bing drew his finger down the Pacific Northwest and across the expanse of blue to China. He felt trapped, as if the lines of longitude and latitude formed a wall between him and freedom.

Fortuneteller's stones were on the altar beside an urn filled with incense. Bing avoided the eyes of the gods who gazed down at him and reached for a stone.

"Little One, so glad you've come."

Bing turned around.

"Shouldn't you be at work?" Fortuneteller asked.

"That's where I'm going now. I lost the stone you gave me, so I need another one."

Fortuneteller thought for a moment and nodded toward the altar. "Then take one."

"Thank you, Uncle," Bing said, taking a stone.

"James said you visited Ba today. What's making him sick?"

"He has a burning fever but sleeps under six blankets because he feels cold. He shivers, and yet this is the hottest month of the year. His face is pale and green. He can't keep food down, keeps coughing and retching."

"Can you cure him? I'll pay you!"

"No, Bing. You have to help save him."

"Me? I'm no doctor!"

"Think, Little One. Think. Isn't it strange that your father fell sick after uncovering Shum's bones?"

"Yes. Does Shum's ghost want revenge?"

"Revenge ghosts don't wait before they take action. They have righteous power on their side. They act immediately, before the guilty party can forget. This isn't a revenge ghost."

"Then why is he making my father sick?"

"I've thought about this. I believe Shum's spirit wants to return home. Your father dug up his bones but couldn't send them back to China because of the missing skull. That's why Shum's spirit refuses to lie still now. He's making your father sick because he wants his help."

"But we don't know where the skull is. Ba checked the grave thoroughly. Twelve years have passed, and nobody knows anything about that man. It's too late!"

"No. Not so."

"Why not?"

"Shum's ghost knows the skull is nearby; otherwise it wouldn't bother your father. You have to look for the skull."

"It's not my job!"

"Then your father will die, Loan Shark will seize you as repayment of the debt, and you'll become a slave in a gambling hall!"

# Chapter Twelve

B ING STOOD BY THE PICKET FENCE AND GAZED UP AT THE BENTLEY HOUSE, TINTED RED BY THE SETTING SUN.

He entered the house through the back door. The kitchen was deserted. He tiptoed to the dining room door and saw Mrs. Bentley sitting at the table alone. There were half-empty plates in front of her. Her shoulders were slumped over, and, for a moment, Bing felt sorry for her.

"Look who crawled in," she sneered, looking up at Bing.

Mrs. Moore hurried in with an empty baby bottle. "Oh. The boy is back."

"Our faithful servant, the coward. It must be time for his dinner," Mrs. Bentley said, rising from her chair. "But he's probably too scared to eat."

The housekeeper looked at Bing and sighed, as Mrs. Bentley left the room. Mrs. Moore's face was grey, and strands of hair had slipped loose from her bun.

"You can't work here with those dirty hands," she said. "Go wash yourself right away."

Bing felt relieved. He cleaned his face and hands, then changed his clothes and made sure his new stone from Fortuneteller was safe in his pocket.

At the kitchen sink, Mrs. Moore was pouring warm milk into the baby's bottle.

"I'll take that up." Bing held out his hand.

"They're in Mr. Bentley Sr.'s room," said Mrs. Moore.

"But why?" Bing blurted out in surprise.

*Isn't Mrs. Bentley scared to be in that room?* he wondered.

"Don't ask foolish questions. Are you going up or not?"

Bing paused for half a second and thought, *I have to go up. I can't afford to be afraid any more.*

Mrs. Bentley did not look up as Bing entered Mr. Bentley Sr.'s room and delivered the milk.

When he returned to the kitchen, Mrs. Moore had supper ready for him.

"All I have are hard-boiled eggs, potatoes and pickled beets," she said. "I've not had any time to cook. And don't mind what Mrs. Bentley said when you came back. She's still shaken up from this afternoon."

"Did she say what happened in the parlour?"

"No," said Mrs. Moore, staring into her teacup.

"Do you believe in ghosts?"

"I attend church every Sunday."

"So is that yes or no?" Bing frowned.

"I'll tell you a story my grandmother told me."

*When she was a young woman living in a small village in northern England, my grandmother's best friend, Beatrice, married a widower, a man whose wife and baby had died during the birth.*

*At first, Beatrice didn't want to marry the man, because she knew he and his first wife had been childhood sweethearts. But the man yearned for children, so he pursued Beatrice with determination.*

*A year after her marriage to the widower, Beatrice gave birth to a very healthy child. Man and wife were overjoyed. But after a few months, the child became very ill. He had fevers and chills, and his hair fell out in clumps. Beatrice asked all the village women for advice. She used all the tried and true remedies they recommended. But her baby only got sicker and sicker.*

*Late one night, while Beatrice dozed beside her baby's crib, she suddenly glanced up and looked into the mirror. By the light of the flickering candle, she saw the stony face of her husband's first wife. Beatrice screamed and the face vanished.*

*She told her story to her husband, but he advised her to get more rest. She told her story to the pastor at church, but he shrugged her off.*

*Finally, Beatrice went to the hunchback woman who lived alone in a hut deep in the forest. She was the one the farmers called upon when their animals were sick, badly injured or about to give birth.*

*The old woman listened to Beatrice and said, "Here is what you must do. Tomorrow night, when the moon is full, go to the graveyard and dig up your husband's first child. Open the coffin and remove the silver cross from the baby's neck. Take the cross you wear on your neck and place it in the coffin. Close the lid and rebury the child. Then place the cross from the dead child around your son's neck. From then on, I promise, your little one will have no problems."*

*The next evening, Beatrice slipped into the graveyard and did exactly as she was told, even though her entire body trembled as she dug open the*

*grave. The next day, her child began to recover and*
*soon grew big and strong. She made him vow to*
*always wear that cross, and to his dying day, he kept*
*that promise.*

Bing's hands went cold as he reached into his pocket and pulled out James' cross. "Did it look like this?"
Mrs. Moore nodded.

The next morning, Mrs. Moore handed Bing a tray of empty pickle jars. "Put these away in the attic and don't break any!"

Bing trudged up the stairs to the attic. The low ceiling and inward-sloping walls made him feel tall. Sunshine flooded in the windows. Bing sidestepped crates and trunks, chairs with worn seats and dusty little tables. In one corner, flowers lay drying on the floor. Large thin shapes leaned against the wall, under canvas sheets. Bing lifted one of the sheets and saw a painting of men and women picnicking on grass, surrounded by chubby angels. Under another was a tall, circular saw blade. Under other sheets were bigger blades. The shelf was crammed with jars without lids, orphaned dishes and kitchen gadgets.

As Bing put the jars on the shelf, his cuff caught a cup handle. It landed on the floor and shattered. Bing swiftly retrieved the pieces and looked for something to wrap them in. He took a long tube of paper from a wicker basket and unrolled it. The deep blue sheets had white lines on them. In the lower corner of the drawing were a neatly printed name and a bold signature: *Robert B. Bentley Sr.*

*This is a drawing of the Bentley house!* Bing realized. *The windows, porch railings and chimneys are identical to the ones I've seen from the road. So Mr. Bentley Sr. must have designed this house!*

"Bing!" Mrs. Moore called. "Where are you?"

"Coming!" He quickly re-rolled the drawing. As he plunged the tube back into the basket, he spotted a stack of newspapers. The first three were *Vancouver News-Advertisers* from 1894. They were all the same edition; so he grabbed a section and wrapped up the broken china. Then he hid the package, just in case Mrs. Moore came up.

The housekeeper marched him out to the shed in the back.

"Bring out the long ladder and wash the conservatory windows," she said.

Bing wrung out soapy cloths and climbed to the top of the windows. Mrs. Moore returned with a bucket of clean water.

*Ka - lang!*

The two of them ducked instinctively at the sound of breaking glass.

"What was that?" Bing yelped.

"It came from the other side of the house."

Bing climbed down the ladder and followed Mrs. Moore into the kitchen. The windows there were solid and intact. They headed upstairs. In the water closet, a window had shattered. Jagged glass lay strewn over the floor.

"This is terrible!" Mrs. Moore gasped, gripping her crucifix.

Bing stepped over the broken glass and peered out the window. "Did someone throw something in?"

"I don't see anything," Mrs. Moore said, scrutinizing the floor.

Bing peered under the tub and behind the washstand. Nothing. No rocks. No bricks.

"What happened?" Mrs. Bentley asked, suddenly appearing at the door.

"The window shattered, Ma'am," replied Mrs. Moore.

"But how?"

*The ghost!* Bing thought.

"I'm not sure, Ma'am," Mrs. Moore answered.

Mrs. Bentley shut her eyes and pursed her lips. "Clean this up," she said.

As she turned to leave, she glanced at Bing and asked, "Are you still afraid?"

"Not any more."

"Good," she said and left.

"How is it that you're not afraid anymore?" asked Mrs. Moore, looking at him curiously.

Bing shrugged.

The housekeeper persisted. "How did you suddenly become so brave? I saw you run away in terror yesterday. I'm surprised you ever came back."

"I had to come back. I need the money."

"Do you know anyone in Chinatown that could help us?"

At first Bing didn't understand and looked blankly at her.

She repeated her question and added, "Bing, something must have happened when you went home to give you the courage to come back. Whatever it was, we could use the same kind of help."

"But I'm Chinese, and you're not."

"Are your ghosts any different from ours?"

Bing was taken aback by Mrs. Moore's question. "When our family elders die, their spirits stay close by. They still want to be part of the family, to see their sons and daughters and grandsons and granddaughters do well. When we pay homage and show respect for our ancestors' deeds, they help us if they can. If we don't, they might come back to bother us."

"Like our ghost?"

"Yes."

"I'm afraid, Bing, very afraid. And Mrs. Bentley is also very scared. Will you go back to Chinatown and find a way to help us?"

Bing shook his head doubtfully.

"I'll pay you, Bing," Mrs. Moore added. "I'll pay you well. Just go to Chinatown and ask around."

# Chapter Thirteen

INSTEAD OF CUTTING THROUGH THE SAWMILL DISTRICT TO CHINATOWN, BING TOOK A DIFFERENT ROAD. HE HAD BEEN CAUTIONED AGAINST GOING INTO THIS PART OF TOWN, BECAUSE NO CHINESE WOULD BE AROUND TO HELP HIM IF TROUBLE AROSE. BUT HE KNEW THIS ROUTE WOULD LOOP AROUND TO FORTUNETELLER'S BUILDING AND LET HIM ENTER IT UNSEEN.

*If the men in Chinatown knew I was going this way,* Bing thought, *they would think I was careless. They would say that children who grow up in Canada don't listen to the wisdom of their elders, that Chinese-Canadian children can't even read or write Chinese, and that they're like empty salmon cans— shiny on the outside, but nothing inside!*

Bing passed workers' hotels, warehouses, drinking saloons and small shops. He walked slowly, peering into the shop windows, and saw a printer guiding wide sheets of paper through a well-oiled press. Through another shop window he saw two barrel-makers, one who hammered at an anvil to make steel hoops and another who trimmed wooden staves to make watertight barrels.

Finally, Bing knocked at Fortuneteller's door and entered.

"You again, Little One?" asked the old man, looking up from his chair. "What do you need now?"

"My employer sent me this time."

Fortuneteller's eyebrows arched.

Bing took a deep breath and told how the ghost had chased the buyers from the house, spooked Mrs. Bentley and pitched a heavy spittoon across the floor at him. He ended with the account of the bathroom window shattering for no apparent reason that morning.

"Wah!" Fortuneteller exclaimed. "A powerful ghost, indeed. So that's why you came yesterday for another stone."

"Do you think I can defeat this ghost? "

"Ghosts can't be defeated; they need to be calmed. Spirits who return to the human world are seeking something very important. Once they find it, peace will be restored. Do you know who this ghost is?"

"It's probably Mr. Bentley Sr.," replied Bing, "Can you sell me something that would protect my employers from him?"

At the very least, Bing wanted to bring home a charm so that Mrs. Moore would pay him. Then he could give some money to Broken-leg and start settling Ba's debts.

"How about a picture of the ghost-fighter god?" Bing asked. "Or one of those word spells?"

He pointed to the table where squares of yellow paper lay, along with crimson ink and several bamboo brushes.

Fortuneteller shook his head.

"Could you give my employer a magic stone then?"

The old man snorted derisively.

"Isn't there anything we can try? Something simple, maybe? Please! This family is in trouble: the husband's out of town, the wife is distraught and wants to sell the house."

"You can help them, Little One."

"They think I'm a coward," he said, still smarting from Mrs. Bentley's remark.

"Doesn't matter what they think. Bing, are you afraid?"

"No!"

"Then you must go back and help the restless ghost find peace. Understand?" Then Fortuneteller's voice softened. "Have you visited your father today?"

Bing shook his head.

"And what have you done to help your father find Shum's skull?"

"Nothing," confessed Bing.

"Your father has been out of his sick-bed looking for it. You should be ashamed. Go to him quickly. Show him respect."

Bing was at the door when Fortuneteller called out, "Remember those stones I gave you? They have no magic. They are just ordinary stones. They didn't help you face the ghosts. You did that by yourself."

Bing went straight to his father's room and found James there.

"What are you doing here?" Bing asked, surprised.

"Uncle Won asked me to bring your father something to eat. He's too sick to come downstairs."

Ba lay under so many blankets that his legs made no ridges under the heavy pile. His cheekbones stuck out from his gaunt face.

James took a spoonful of watery rice from a bowl and tried to push it into Ba's mouth.

"His appetite is poor. He won't eat," James said.

"I'm not hungry. Why are you here, Little One? You should be working," Ba said weakly.

"My boss sent me here on an errand. I can't stay long," Bing answered.

"Now you're here, I'll come back later," James said.

"Wait a minute! Fortuneteller just told me that the stones he gave me are meaningless. Did you know that?"

James nodded.

"Why didn't you tell me?"

"Why would I do that? You needed something to believe in when you went to that house."

"You tricked me."

"It was for your own good."

"Take this back!" Bing said holding out the cross. "I don't need this any more."

James pocketed it without a word and left.

"Have you found Shum's skull yet?" Bing asked Ba.

Ba's eyes flashed. He tried to sit up but started coughing instead. "Who told you that I was out looking for it? Damn that Won-brother; he's got such a big mouth."

"It wasn't Uncle Won. It was Fortuneteller, and he told me that you won't get better until you find it."

"Don't I know that?" Ba's head fell back. "But where can I look? Yesterday, I dragged myself out of bed and crawled to the Wing Sang store. I thought Old Yip would know about that fellow Shum. But he didn't."

"Is there another graveyard?"

"No."

"Is there a spot in the graveyard for missing bones?"

"No."

"What about the Shum family association?"

"Shum is a small surname here. Few of them came to this city, so no family association was ever formed. Nobody bothers about their affairs."

"You should have visited every store in Chinatown and asked about Shum."

"Don't tell me what to do!" snapped Ba.

As Bing strode to the door, Ba called out, "Listen to me. As soon as I die, you have to run as fast as you can to the Chan family association. Tell them you want to go back to China."

The words caught Bing off guard and stung him.

"What about Loan Shark?" Bing asked. "We still owe him money."

"Don't worry. Our family association will deal with him. That's what the organization is there for—to protect all its members."

As Bing reached for the doorknob, he heard his father sigh. "I haven't been a good father, have I? My failures will follow you. I realize that. When people ask who your father was, tell them he never taught you anything. Or tell them he abandoned his family."

Another fit of coughing wracked Ba. "Board a ship and go home. Tell your mother I regret everything. I caused her and your grandmother to lose all hope for a better future.

The villagers will ridicule our family, I know, and there is no one to blame but me."

"You should never have gambled," Bing said hotly. "If you had kept your job at the sawmill and saved your money, we'd have no trouble. Look at Lee Dat. He came to Canada and earned lots of money! Look at Uncle Won. He runs a business and people come to him for help. But you! All you do is dig yourself deeper and deeper into bad luck!"

Ba let out a weary breath before continuing. "When I arrived here, long before your birth, I never gambled. I was careful with money and counted my savings every night. Every morning, I awoke afraid of being fired from my job and not having food to eat. I was sick with worry. But still I went to work. Every penny I earned was sent home, and still I thought it wasn't enough. When my friends invited me to a restaurant, I always refused. When they pulled me into a game of chance, I crossed my arms and wouldn't play. They all laughed at me: said I had no nerve, said I was shyer than a new bride, said I didn't act like a man. One of them even claimed I spread a dark cloud of worry and bad luck wherever I went.

"One day, I found two coins on the road, picked them up, took them to a game-hall and played fan-tan. To my delight, I won. I bet my winnings again, and I won another time. All night long, I kept winning game after game. It was the luckiest day of my life. I left the hall with my pockets full of money. I sent it home and my mother arranged a marriage. The girl she picked was your mother.

"After that, I stopped worrying. What a relief! I realized I wasn't the only one responsible for feeding the family. Chance played a role in my life, and so did the gods of good fortune and bad luck. I felt younger and lighter, as if I had found a new beginning. I stopped worrying. I never got sick again. I sailed home, married your mother and came back here. When you were born, I was sure my luck would continue to improve. I grew more confident and began to take greater risks. I put money into a business, but my partners swindled me. But I didn't lose faith, and I invested again. This time I earned enough for another trip home. On the return trip, I brought you with me, so you could grow up in a land of opportunity.

"Then I started to lose at gambling. My luck had changed, but I refused to believe it. I couldn't give up the hope of bettering your life; so I started borrowing money. And the more I borrowed, the more I lost. And now I've lost everything."

"No, you haven't," Bing said, trembling and looking into his father's eyes. "You have a son to help you."

"Then go back to your job. I'll be fine. Something will work out."

On his way back to the Bentley house, Bing leaned against the railing on the Cambie Bridge to let the breeze from the creek cool him. The sawmills along the waterfront stretched west as far as his eyes could see. Booms of dark logs floated close to shore. Clouds of smoke billowed from burning sawdust, and the buzz of saws drifted across the water.

*If Ba dies,* he thought, *then it's up to me to take care of Mother and Grandmother.*

He imagined them entering the village with weary faces and dusty black smocks, their carrying poles laden with tawny sheaves of ripened rice. He imagined the sound of their voices calling him and heard them beat the rice sheaves on the stone courtyard to loosen the grains.

*I'll send money home so everyone in the village will show Ma and Grandma proper respect,* he told himself.

Bing reached into his pocket and pulled out Fortuneteller's stone. He drew his arm back and hurled the rock high into the sky. It fell into the distant water.

On Fairview Hill, workers were installing power poles along the new avenues. Holes had been dug, and teams of horses strained at ropes and pulleys attached to tall wooden frames bracing against each pole. The poles stood an equal distance from each other, and Bing wished his life were just as orderly.

He was watching a pole sway into place when he bumped into someone.

"Sorry," he mumbled.

A hand grabbed Bing's shirt and yanked it, popping several buttons. "Watch where you're going, Chinaboy!"

It was the man in the red-checked shirt. Red Checks' friend, Charlie, came up behind Bing.

Bing pulled away, but Charlie pushed Bing back into Red Checks' grip. Both men smelled of whiskey and stale sweat.

"I said I was sorry! Let me go!" Bing tugged at the hand holding him.

"Sure!" Red Checks said and suddenly released his grip.

Bing sprawled backward. He scrambled to his feet and swung at Red Checks. But Red Checks grabbed Bing's fists in his enormous hands.

"I let you go," Red Checks chortled. "But you're back!"

Bing kicked out in vain. Then his arms were yanked up and he was lifted off his feet. He kicked harder, but to no avail.

"Hey, we got ourselves a wee yellow kitten here!" hooted the other man. "Let's hear him meow!"

"Hey, Charlie, get a sack and we'll toss him into the creek." Red Checks laughed.

"Let me go!" Bing twisted to one side to aim his kicks better, but Charlie danced in and out, slapping Bing's cheeks. Then he smacked Bing's nose and pummelled his upper body.

"Turn him upside down!" Charlie laughed.

Red Checks reached for Bing's feet, but Bing landed a solid kick.

"Yow!" shouted Red Checks in pain.

"I know! Take off his pants," Charlie said.

He moved in carefully, dodging Bing's kicking legs. Then a voice called out from behind them. "Let the boy go!"

Bing saw Mrs. Bentley moving quickly toward them. She waved her closed parasol at them and shouted, "Did you hear me? I said to let the boy go!"

Red Checks swung around, using Bing as a shield. Mrs. Bentley swung her parasol at them but missed.

"Let him go," she repeated. "Do as I say! I'm warning you. I'll report you both to the police. I know your names."

Red Checks paused for a moment and then heaved Bing into the bushes. Bing rolled over and sat up. His attackers had run off.

# Chapter Fourteen

T HAT NIGHT, BING COULDN'T SLEEP. EVERY TIME HE SHUT HIS EYES, RED CHECKS LUNGED AT HIM. BING WISHED HE WERE BACK IN CHINA, WITH ITS FLAT ROLLING PLAINS, IRRIGATED FIELDS AND DIKES FANNING OUT FROM ANCIENT RIVERS. HE FELT SAFE THERE. LIFE WAS SIMPLE. THE HILLS WERE EASILY CLIMBED IN A MORNING'S TREK, AND THE VILLAGES OF BLACK-BRICK HOUSES WERE GUARDED BY STURDY STONE TOWERS. HE FELT PROTECTED BY THE VERY LANDSCAPE ITSELF: THE GROVES OF ORANGE TREES, THE FARMS AND THE COILING RIVERS.

*But perhaps there is something protecting me here as well,* Bing thought. *Mrs. Bentley could have walked by and let Red Checks and his friend beat me to death. But she didn't. I have*

*to find a way to repay her. She saved my life, so I am indebted
to her. I must solve the problem of the Bentley ghost!*

The next morning, when Bing went upstairs, Mrs.
Moore was already at work.

"Make toast," she commanded. "Two slices for Mrs.
Bentley and then enough for you and me. We've got to get
the house ready."

Bing held the toasting grill over the stove. The dry wood
in the stove crackled and popped, and Bing recalled how
his mother and grandmother used to burn ghost money and
paper clothes to send to the ancestral spirits.

*Maybe I can send Mr. Bentley Sr.'s ghost an offering
through the fire,* Bing mused.

"Mrs. Bentley said your shirt needed mending," said
Mrs. Moore. "Give it to me and I'll darn it."

"No thank you. I'll fix it myself."

"You sew?"

"Yes, Ma'am."

"When you're finished, go clean up the shed," Mrs.
Moore said.

Later that morning, Bing heard a wagon approach. He
walked out of the shed and saw a wagon standing in the
driveway, its horse calmly grazing. The sign on its side-
panel read *Wright and Sons, Glaziers: window repairs done
right!*

*The house seems at peace today,* Bing thought.

Bing watched a tradesman carry a pane of glass into the kitchen entrance. He went back into the shed to finish cleaning. Then he decided to see if the man needed any help. He found the tradesman in the water closet cutting glass.

"Hey, boy," the tradesman said, looking up. "You're just in time. Hold this for me while I set the putty. What's your name?"

Bing told him, and the man said, "I'm Mr. Wright, the glazier."

As Mr. Wright lifted a pane of glass to replace the water closet window, Bing asked, "Did you know Mr. Bentley Sr.?"

"A fine man. But very impatient, always in a rush. He started out in life without a penny, you know, and no one expected him to succeed. But look at this house. Solid as stone, built from the finest lumber. When I installed the original glass, the inside walls were going up and wiring was being strung. He came every day, early in the morning, and stayed long after the workmen were gone. He even came on Sundays."

"Have you heard there's a ghost in this house?"

"Hush, boy, nobody is supposed to know."

Before Bing could ask more questions, Mrs. Moore called. "Bing! Don't bother the tradesman. Go and weed the garden."

Reluctantly, he headed off and squatted by the flowerbeds. On the street, children ran by, rattling sticks against the picket fence. Bing looked up and followed them with his eyes for a second. When he looked down again, he saw a smooth stone with words chiselled into it.

---

LAID ON MAY 22, 1903, TO THE GLORY OF GOD,
BY HIS HUMBLE SERVANT
ROBERT BERNARD BENTLEY, SENIOR
*A HOUSE TO HONOUR HIM FOREVER*

---

Bing's fingers traced the words. The house was only four years old. *Old Mr. Bentley must have loved it greatly to install such a fancy stone like this. Stone will last forever, but human beings don't. Too bad Mr. Bentley Sr. died before he could enjoy it,* Bing thought.

Then a sudden thought excited him. *That's why his spirit is not at peace! It's this house! He designed it; his mill cut the wood. He wanted to live here a long time and never expected to die in an accident. No wonder his ghost has come back.*

Now Bing knew what he needed to do in order to satisfy Mr. Bentley Sr.'s ghost.

In the shed, he found thin bamboo poles and string used for staking plants. He took them to the kitchen, where he gathered the needle, thread and scissors that he had used to mend his shirt. He took everything to the basement, and then he headed upstairs, as quietly as possible. On the second floor, he heard women's voices in the main bedroom.

Once in the attic, Bing went straight to the blueprint drawing of the house. Bing took two sheets showing the four sides of the exterior of the house and returned to the basement with them. Then he called Mrs. Moore into the kitchen.

"I have a plan," he said. "To bring peace to the house."

"But yesterday you said nobody could help us."

"I'm going to make an offering to Mr. Bentley Sr. in order to show him respect."

"Is there any way I can help?"

"Yes. Please keep Mrs. Bentley out of Mr. Bentley Sr.'s room for the rest of the day."

She nodded emphatically.

He immediately returned to his room, unrolled the drawings and cut out the four sides of the house. He laid the bamboo beside them and sliced the sticks to match. These he made into a four-sided frame, tying each corner with string. Then he fastened each side of the house, cut from the drawing, to the sides of the frame. He laced the four sides into a square and tied them together at the corners. Finally, he bent together the top edges of the paper and roughly sewed them together to make a roof. He had built a blue paper model of the house.

Bing took it up to Mr. Bentley Sr.'s room without being seen. He removed a photograph of Mr. Bentley Sr. from the wall and set it on the fireplace mantle. Then he lit one of the candles he had taken from home and set it on a saucer next to the photo.

"Mr. Robert Bernard Bentley, Sr.," Bing whispered, holding up the blue model in front of the picture. "Mr. Bentley Sr., come and look at your beautiful house. It is magnificent, and I will send it to you tonight. Please come, look at it now."

Just as Bing placed the model on a coffee table directly in front of the photo, he thought he smelled cigar smoke again. He shut the door and crept downstairs.

The rest of the day went by quickly. There were two bushels of apples to peel for making pies and sauce. After his dinner chores were completed, Bing slipped back upstairs into Mr. Bentley Sr.'s room.

The door squeaked as Bing entered the room and glanced nervously around. There was no time to waste. The candle had burnt out, so Bing lit a fresh one and added another to the other side of the portrait. They cast a soft glow and threw dancing shadows onto the wall.

Then he lifted the model of the house and held it in front of the photo again.

"This is for you, Mr. Bentley Sr.," he said, as loudly as he dared. "You designed and built a beautiful house. You should have been able to enjoy it for a long time. And now I will send this model to you, so you can have your house in the spirit world. You don't have to keep coming back here."

Bing dipped one corner of the house into the candle and the flame ignited the paper. Quickly, he knelt and slipped the burning model into the fireplace. White and black smoke billowed out as flames consumed the bamboo stakes.

Bing shut his eyes. "Go," he urged the burning house. "Go to Mr. Bentley Sr. now. Travel to the spirit world and bring him peace."

"What's going on here?" Mrs. Bentley shouted.

Bing jumped to his feet and saw her standing in the doorway with her hands pressed over her mouth. She looked horrified.

"You can't practise your heathen rituals here!" Mrs. Bentley gasped, pointing a trembling hand at the blaze. "You're fired! Take your things and leave."

Rest in Peace

# Chapter Fifteen

IT WAS DUSK WHEN BING REACHED CHINATOWN. IN BA'S ROOM, UNCLE WON WAS BENDING OVER THE SICK MAN.

"Bing-wing, you came at the right time!" exclaimed the proprietor. "I was just about to take your father to hospital. You speak better English. So you take him. Red Hare is already hitched to a wagon."

"Hospital?"

"Your father is much worse. He coughed all night, so loudly that the drivers couldn't sleep. This morning, when Sing-brother took him some soup, your Ba kept vomiting. He's nothing but skin and bones."

Uncle Won shook his head. "The drivers think he'll die soon, and they don't want it happening here."

"You think he's going to die?"

"Hard to say. When someone is so sick, who can tell if he'll live or die? At the hospital, the doctors will know."

"Do they let in Chinese?"

"They should."

"I'll have to pay the doctors."

Uncle Won reached into his pocket.

"I'll lend you some money." He handed Bing several bills, more than he had ever held in his life.

"I'll repay you as soon as I get paid," said Bing. He was ashamed to admit that he had been fired.

They wrapped Ba in a blanket, carried him downstairs and lifted him onto a wagon lined with straw and blankets. Ba seemed barely awake, though he moaned every now and then. His face had a greenish tinge to it. Clearly, Shum's ghost had seized control over Ba's body.

"Be careful," called out Uncle Won, as Bing drove away. "Gangs of troublemakers have been coming into town from Bellingham. They're parading tomorrow to cause problems for the Chinese."

Atop Fairview Hill, Bing turned west onto Broadway. A half-moon illuminated the imposing three-storey edifice of the hospital. As Bing urged Red Hare on, he could see the narrow, grey stone towers rising above a long, flat roof. Closer, he saw that ambulances waited near the main entrance.

Bing climbed into the back of the wagon and woke his father.

"Ba, we've arrived. Ba, get up."

"Where are we?" Ba's eyes flickered open.

"At the hospital."

"Hospital? Have you brought me here to die?"

"No, the doctors here will make you better."

Ba's head turned from side to side. "Where's my wife? And my mother? Can't I say a few words to them?"

"Sit up, Ba," pleaded Bing. "Climb off the wagon. I'll walk you in."

"My legs are too weak. I have no strength."

As Bing helped his father off the wagon, Ba fell to the ground with a loud moan.

A nurse wearing a stiff white uniform ran over with a lamp. "Do you need help?"

"My father is sick," Bing said.

"Don't move him! Let me get a stretcher!" she exclaimed.

Relieved, Bing wiped the saliva from his father's chin.

Two attendants came out and lifted Ba onto a stretcher. Inside, the nurse stopped Bing as the men carried his father into the basement.

"You have to wait here," the nurse said, handing him Ba's blanket. "No one is allowed in the examining room."

"Will he be all right?"

"Only the doctor can say. Sit here. I'll be back to ask you some questions."

Bing tucked the blanket under his arm and looked around the lobby. Wooden benches surrounded a receptionist's desk. A handful of people sat waiting. Bing noticed the strong smell of bleach and lye in the corridor.

Each time a doctor passed by him, Bing glanced up. One doctor frowned and gave him a stern look. Bing assumed it was because he was Chinese.

Nurses brought out a young man on crutches, his legs wrapped in bandages. His family helped him walk out of the hospital.

Bing felt a lump in his throat. *Will the nurses bring Ba out healthy and hardy again?* he wondered.

Bing found it hard to sit still. The lobby opened into several long corridors, each lined with doors. A sign saying *Examining Rooms* pointed to the right-hand corridor. A nurse emerged and summoned a patient to follow her. An orderly hurried by with a tray of dark bottles. A doctor came from the examining rooms.

*That's strange,* Bing thought. *They took Ba downstairs, but the examining rooms are up here.*

Bing went over and looked down the stairwell where the attendants had taken Ba, but it was deserted. *Perhaps Ba was taken to the basement because he's Chinese,* Bing thought. Then he returned to his seat in the corridor.

On the wall facing him were rows of framed photographs. Bing thought he recognized one and went over to look at it more closely. It was the same photograph he had seen in Mr. Bentley Sr.'s room—*The Inaugural Board Meeting of Vancouver Hospital, 1891*.

Just then, the nurse returned and led Bing into an office. She asked Ba's name, his age, his home address, how long he had lived in Canada and whether or not he spoke English.

"What is your father's occupation?"

Bing hesitated. "Gravedigger."

"What seems to be the matter with him?"

"He's hot and then he's cold. He won't eat and throws up. He's weak and can't walk. He coughs all night long."

"Poor boy, it's hard to see your father sick, isn't it?"

Bing looked away.

"Has your father seen a doctor?" she asked.

"Only in Chinatown."

"What has your father's health been like in the past?"

"He's never sick!"

"We need to wait until tomorrow to run some tests. Come back then. We'll know more at that time."

"Can I see him before I go?"

"No. Come back tomorrow."

"How much do I have to pay?"

"We won't know until he's been examined."

"The sign in the hall says the examining room is down this corridor, but the men took my father downstairs. Did they take him to the right place?"

"Yes, of course. All Oriental patients go downstairs."

"Why?"

"That's the rule. So they can receive the appropriate care. Now go home. I'm very busy."

*I bet no one's looking after Ba,* Bing thought bitterly. *The hospital puts Chinese people downstairs, so they'll be out of sight.*

He was determined to say goodbye to Ba and headed to the stairway. But a uniformed watchman grabbed his arm.

"Boy, you're going the wrong way."

The guard marched him to the front door.

*Even if I sneaked into the basement, where would I find Ba?* Bing sighed helplessly.

"Hey, Bing-wing Chan!" a deep voice called in English. "Come! Follow me."

Bing turned around and saw a man beckoning to him. He was standing on the landing between the ground and second floors.

"Are you calling me?" Bing asked.

The man nodded. Bing ran over and followed him up the stairs to the second floor and down the dimly lit hallway. Bing looked around and saw a nearby door ajar. The electric lights were on, so he peeked in.

It was a classroom with blackboards at the front, tall windows to one side and rows of wooden chairs with writing tables attached. At one end of the room stood a wooden cabinet with glass doors. As Bing approached the cabinet, he saw rows of human skulls.

*Shum's head!* Bing thought.

The skulls were resting in wooden trays, and each tray was labelled. The skulls were smooth and clean. Some were shiny and golden, while others were dull and patched with brown. Bing stared at the eye sockets, at the hollows where noses once had been and at the openings that were mouths. Some had plates of teeth wired in place; others were empty. Two small skulls had labels that read *Male, Caucasian, New Westminster, age 9, received 1894* and *Female, Native Indian, Stanley Park, age 12, received 1902*.

Bing bent down and checked all the labels. None on the bottom shelf were Chinese, nor the second, nor the third. But there it was on the fourth shelf, neatly written in black ink: *Male, Chinese, New Westminster, age 29, received 1895.*

*That's the correct year!* Bing thought.

He had found Shum's skull! He could scarcely believe it. Now he had to act quickly.

"Mr. Shum, I have to take your skull. Please, I hope you don't mind. I'll be very careful with it."

With great care, Bing lifted the tray containing Shum's skull. It seemed to weigh no more than a basket woven from straw. He noticed a file folder on the tray under the skull.

Bing took several deep breaths and wrapped the tray, containing both the folder and the skull, in the blanket. He then walked back into the corridor. It was empty. And so were the stairs at the other end of the hallway.

He hurried down to the basement and was struck by the dank smell, which hung in the air. No one was in sight. Then he spotted a hand-written sign on a door that read *Ward for Orientals* and hurried inside.

"Ba!"

His father lay in bed, a small lamp on the table beside him. The room had no windows, just a row of empty beds and shelves with nothing on them.

"Bing-wing, is that you?" Ba raised his head. "What are you doing here?"

"Ba, you look better." His father's face had regained some colour and his eyes were brighter. When he took Ba's hand, it felt warm. "Have they given you any medicine?"

Ba sat up. "They haven't given me anything yet. But I feel much better, and I want to go home."

"I found Shum's skull! It was in a classroom upstairs," Bing said, holding out the bundle with the skull.

Ba took the bundle and held it carefully.

"I'll be fine now!" he exclaimed, swinging his legs off the bed. "Now that we have the skull, my life is restored."

Ba handed the bundle back to Bing, wrapped a dressing gown around himself and quickly opened the door. Cautiously, the two of them stepped into the corridor.

"Hush, someone's coming," Bing whispered.

A watchman was making his rounds.

"Who's there?" the watchman called. He peered down the hallway at them.

Bing backed against the door.

"What're you doing there?" called the watchman. He was coming closer.

Just then Bing caught a sudden whiff of cigar smoke.

"Help!" screamed the watchman, bolting in the opposite direction.

"Whose ghost was that?" Ba shivered.

"I'll explain later. Let's get out of here fast."

# Chapter Sixteen

"WE CAN'T GO TO THE CEMETERY NOW!" SHOUTED BING OVER THE ROAR OF WHEELS AND GALLOPING HOOVES. HE CLUNG TO HIS SEAT TO STAY ABOARD THE WILDLY LURCHING WAGON.

*I should never have let Ba drive,* he thought.

"Shum's skull must be reunited with the bones as soon as possible," Ba hollered. "We have to show respect to Shum."

"But we don't have any shovels! How can we dig up the bones?"

"A ghost that buries two shovels five feet deep can certainly provide a shovel if it wants. Just wait and see."

Bing shuddered at the memory of the vanishing shovels, but was relieved to see that Ba was right. When they reached the gravesite, an old shovel was lying there. Moonlight gleamed along its polished wooden handle.

"Let's get to work," Ba said.

"No Ba, you rest. I'll dig."

Because he already knew where the bones were and because he only needed to reach the top of the bundle to yank it out, Bing thought the digging would go quickly. Still, he had to dig carefully around the bones to avoid stepping on them.

Soon Bing struck the top of the knotted white cloth Ba had buried just days before. Bing pulled at the knot, but the packed earth refused to budge.

"Don't pull at the bundle!" Ba shouted. "Dig the whole thing out!"

Bing yanked hard; but this time the cloth ripped and he fell backward.

"Stupid fool," Ba shouted. "Didn't I tell you not to pull?"

*There's the old Ba back again*, Bing thought.

"Now you have to pick up the bones one by one," Ba taunted.

Bing stared at the half-covered bones. The last time he had seen them, they had terrified him. But now he knew that the bones of the dead did not possess great powers. It was their ghosts that did.

"I'm not afraid of the bones, the ghost or you anymore, Ba," Bing said, standing tall in the grave.

"Show your father proper respect!"

"Who was it that saved your life, Ba?"

Ba was speechless.

"So show your son proper respect!" Bing said, reaching down for the bones.

Ba unwrapped the skull and placed it carefully on the ground. He then put the tray back in the wagon and spread out the blanket by the side of the grave.

Bing handed the bones to Ba one at a time and Ba set the bones in the blanket. Bing passed up the fractured ribcage as though it were a delicate rice-paper lantern. After removing the larger bones, Bing tugged gently at the remains of the cloth. This time, the bundle lifted easily.

Ba sorted the bones into neat piles and then properly laid out the skeleton.

"We're missing two pieces of the spine," Ba called out. "Look for them."

Bing sifted through the loose soil. It felt cool and wet and soft. He worked from one side of the pit to the other until he found the missing pieces. Ba carefully fit them in.

Then Bing jumped out of the grave and watched Ba put Shum's skull in its proper place. Father and son took a step back and gazed at the now complete skeleton in the bright moonlight.

"You are whole again, Mr. Shum," Bing whispered. "With your skull back where it belongs, you'll be able to see where you're going. You'll soon be sailing home to China!"

"Now fill in the grave," Ba said. "I'll wrap the skeleton up and put it in the wagon. What should I do about the tray and these papers?"

"Keep them in the wagon."

"What about the shovel?"

"Shum's ghost will have to see to that," Bing laughed, and Ba smiled too.

After replacing the soil, Bing climbed into the wagon. Ba clucked at Red Hare and they headed back to Chinatown. This time, Ba drove slowly.

"Ba, will you stop gambling now?" Bing asked.

Ba didn't answer.

"How long will I have to work to pay off your debts?" Bing asked. "I want to go back to school."

Ba stared straight ahead.

"You think going to school will get you a better life?" Ba asked.

"Look at James. He works in a bank."

"Hah! If business slows down, he'll be the first one fired."

"At least he has a respectable job."

They drove back to Uncle Won's without saying another word to each other. The night sky began to lighten as they turned off Westminster Road. It was dawn. Bing had completely lost track of the time.

It was mid-afternoon when Bing awoke. Ba snored peacefully, in the bunk below. Bing listened to the steady rhythm, a reassuring sign of Ba's recovery.

Bing lay back and wondered if anything had changed in the Bentley house after yesterday's events. Things had certainly changed for him. He still wanted to go back to school, and the fall term had already begun. But first he had to help clear his father's debts. He had to find another job soon.

"Hey, Little One," called Uncle Won, pounding on the door. "You lazy worm! Get up! There's a visitor here to see you! Hurry up!"

Bing rolled out of bed and reached for his clothes.

Downstairs, Mrs. Bentley stood at the front of the store and fanned herself with a newspaper.

"Hello, Bing," she said with a smile. "People at the big store told me I would find you here."

"Is something wrong?"

"I came to thank you. Last night, George slept straight through without waking or crying. And this morning I felt rested and relaxed. I went into my father-in-law's room, and for the first time since his death, it felt warm and friendly. Then Mrs. Moore explained to me what it was you were doing up there yesterday. I was frightened when I saw you burning something, but I understand you were helping us."

Bing jumped in to explain. "I performed a ceremony for Mr. Bentley Sr. He loved his house dearly, and he couldn't bear to see it sold. Chinese people believe they can send things to deceased relatives in the spirit world. We burn ghost money, paper clothes and incense to show our respect for all the ancestors have done for us. When the spirits receive our gifts, they know they are appreciated."

"What did you send my father-in-law?"

"I built a model of his house from the drawings I found in the attic. That's what I burned in his room."

"That's all?"

Bing nodded.

"When I saw the flames and my father-in-law's photograph, I thought you were going to burn his picture!"

"No, I sent him a token of respect."

"Well, it worked!"

"I also wanted to repay you for stopping those hoodlums from attacking me. You saved my life."

"Well, you might have ended up in the hospital. I've never liked bullies or fighting. I came here today to offer you your job back. We'd very much like to have you working for us again. I'm sure my husband would like to meet you."

*That's great!* Bing thought. *I might get boxing lessons from Bulldog after all!*

"Can I start tomorrow?" Bing asked.

"That would be fine." Mrs. Bentley stood and headed for the door. "We look forward to seeing you."

Bing felt a sense of accomplishment. His debt to Mrs. Bentley had been repaid.

The front door opened again, and Uncle Sing came in.

"Hey, Little One, I bought you some bread, freshly steamed!"

Bing ate and slipped out to the stable. He walked around and saw that someone had already carried in feed and water and cleaned the stalls. Red Hare snorted and seemed happy to see him again. When he passed the shed, he smiled. Shum's bones were finally complete. He peeked in and saw the neatly tied bundle from earlier this morning. Beside it was the tray with the file from the hospital cabinet.

Bing scanned the papers. Sketches gave the skull's measurements, while a report compared it to other specimens. A letter on official government stationery stated that the skull had been given to the hospital for teaching purposes. Finally, there was a small newspaper clipping, glued to a sheet of paper. The item had yellowed with age. Its 1897 headline read:

### GRISLY MURDER FINALLY SOLVED
*Yesterday, just before he was scheduled to be executed, the notorious murderer, Jin Dang, showed police officers where in Barnett Forest he had buried the skull of his victim, Chinaman Shum Shek. By means most foul, Dang had beheaded Shum's body to prevent any identification of his victim.*

"I want to send Shum's bones to China today," Ba said, coming into the courtyard, "so that the pain of all these years can begin to heal. I'll build a sturdy crate so they can be shipped off immediately."

Bing looked around. "We'll have to go to the lumberyard. The drivers used up all the wood to build the fence."

Bing harnessed Red Hare to a wagon and they set off for the lumberyard.

Westminster Road was busy with shoppers and children. They crowded around bins of merchandise on the sidewalk under signs. Flyers that read *Parade and Rally, September 7* were posted everywhere along the street.

*That's today,* Bing thought.

After buying the lumber, they headed back to Chinatown. But as they drew nearer, traffic slowed to a crawl. Impatient motorcar drivers honked their horns and deliverymen shouted angrily at each other to clear the way. The smell of gasoline fumes and horse droppings engulfed them. Bing heard a low rumble in the distance. He stood up to see what was causing the delay and saw a large crowd blocking the road ahead. Never before had he seen so many people on the road.

Ba tried to turn Red Hare around, but they were surrounded by other horses and motorcars. He jumped off the wagon and tried leading Red Hare through the crowd. He didn't get very far and finally came back to the wagon. "We have to wait it out," he said.

From behind them, more and more people surged ahead to City Hall. As they passed, Bing felt the wagon shake from side to side.

"This crowd is larger than any I've ever seen. There must be several thousand people here!" Bing said.

"It's just a parade." Ba waved a hand dismissively. "They blow their horns and march up and down a few times and they'll be tired."

Westminster Road was jammed with people, mostly men and teenage boys, all jostling for a clear look at the parade. There was hardly any room for anyone to move.

In front of City Hall, a temporary stage had been set up with chairs and a podium. A backdrop proclaimed *Vancouver Welcomes the Anti-Asiatic League* in large letters.

A marching band passed by the bank, trumpets and horns glinting in the sunlight. The musicians played a patriotic tune, as if this were a day of celebration. A motorcar passed by. Two men sat high in the back, wearing sashes across their chests. They saluted and shouted at the spectators, who responded by wildly waving their caps and straw hats and shouting back.

Next came a line of bagpipe players, their instruments droning melodies, and then a platoon of men dressed in white, with white aprons and white puffy hats. Their sign read *Bakery Workers Union, Local 42. Do You Know Who Makes Your Bread?* Behind the bakers, a pair of horses pulled a large wooden frame with a banner. A man's boot labelled *British Columbia* was kicking a pigtailed Chinese man off a high cliff into the ocean. *Keep Our Province White,* the caption said. The audience cheered and whistled, as the men with the banner smiled and waved.

Above the heads of the crowd, Bing saw the polished tips of dark rifles sail by.

*Soldiers,* he thought fearfully. *And they're not here to protect us.*

Two horses pulled a wagon carrying a hangman's scaffold. From it hung pants and a shirt stuffed with straw, a crude representation of a Chinese man, a pigtail hanging from its head. The straw figure dangled upside-down, suspended by its foot. Three boys took turns swinging baseball bats at the head. Bing recognized one of the boys as Freddie Cox.

He heard loud applause and repeated shouts: "Bravo! Well done, boys! Hit him again!"

The spectators suddenly started chanting, "Kick the Chinese out, give the jobs to us! Kick the Chinese out, give the jobs to us!"

"We have to get back to Uncle Won's. He said there would be big trouble today. I'll try to lead Red Hare back," Bing shouted to Ba over the noise of the angry crowd.

As Bing jumped off the wagon and reached for Red Hare's bridle, he was swept away into the swarming crowd. Without warning, someone grabbed Bing. It was Red Checks and Charlie.

"Well, lookee here," drawled Red Checks. "Who's this?"

Bing tried to get away, but Red Checks held onto him. "Not so fast, monkey-face. You made us look damned foolish in front of that lady last week. Who was she, your fairy godmother? We'll show you a thing or two."

Bing clenched his fists. As Red Checks lunged, Bing threw a solid right jab that flattened Red Check's nose and knocked him into Charlie's arms. Red Checks yelped, his face covered in blood. Bing saw a hole in the crowd and ran through it down Hastings Street.

Just as he reached the corner of Chinatown, he heard a roar explode behind him. He turned to see the crowd change direction and charge at him in a massive wave. Hundreds of men were shouting, screaming, hooting and jeering. They brandished sticks and bats and thrust their fists into the air.

# Chapter Seventeen

"TROUBLE, TROUBLE!" BING SHOUTED, RUNNING INTO UNCLE WON'S STORE.

But no one was there.

*They must be out back with the horses,* Bing thought. *I hope Ba and Red Hare are with them.*

Suddenly, there was a crash of shattering glass. It was store windows down the street. *Crash,* another window disintegrated. *Crash.*

Uncle Won stumbled down the stairs, followed by Uncle Sing, Big Ming and Uncle Yung.

"What's all the noise?" hollered Uncle Won.

"Whites are attacking Chinatown!"

They heard the horses whinnying, and they rushed out into the courtyard. Frantic animals were stamping their feet. The horses lunged from side to side, banging and thumping against their stalls, panicked eyes blazing.

"Let them out!" shouted Uncle Won.

Dent-head opened the stalls; the horses reared and charged into the courtyard.

"Everyone! Get back inside the store!" shouted Uncle Won.

"What about the horses?" Dent-head shouted back.

"They're fine! We need to save our windows!"

They raced back into the store. Uncle Won grabbed a shovel and raised it high.

"If anyone comes in, I'll crack open his head!"

They reached the front just in time to see the windows shatter. The mob on the streets whooped with joy.

Uncle Won and the others stood their ground while Bing ran back into the courtyard. The horses were in a frenzy. He heard a loud, steady pounding on the other side of the fence.

*They're using a log to batter down the fence!* Bing realized. *They want to kill the horses!*

He heard the slam of a battering ram along with men's voices chanting, "Chinks go away! Chinks go away!"

*The shed! The bones!* Bing thought. *I've got to save Shum's bones.*

Bing dashed into the shed and carried out the bundle of bones. At the same time, the battering ram broke through the fence, which gave way with a huge, ripping crash. Dozens of men waving sticks and clubs burst into the courtyard.

Suddenly, the bundle of bones flew out of his hands, and Shum's skeleton rose up out of it. Atop its shoulders, the skull swayed from side to side, shaking with displeasure, and the bony arms reached out like a blind man groping for direction.

The skeleton hurtled toward the mob of white men. They turned and fled back onto the street, pursued by Shum's skeleton and the wild horses.

Bing heard the hollow clatter of metal, as if people were beating on tin pails or banging garbage can lids together. There was a shrill sound of police whistles, followed by an eerie silence.

Then Ba burst into the courtyard atop the wagon pulled by Red Hare.

"Thank the Heavens you're safe," he cried out. "What happened to you? I was so scared!"

The noise on the street had stopped now, and Bing heard the clanging of fire-wagon bells. The riot was over.

Uncle Won strode out to survey the broken fence.

"You weren't here, Tin-brother," said Uncle Won to Ba. "But it's a good thing your son was. He saved your bones from the rioters."

"You did?" exclaimed Ba, jumping down from the wagon and embracing Bing. "You're not afraid of anything any more, not even demented rioters. You saved my life, and I never even thanked you."

Bing pulled away, and saw tears in Ba's eyes.

"I have to take better care of you," Ba said.

Bing swallowed hard and buried his head in the crook of his father's neck. He had never heard Ba speak such words before, nor had he ever expected to. But the moment he heard them, an enormous peace rose up inside him.

Then a voice whispered in Bing's ear, "You helped me, so I helped you." The words were in Chinese.

Bing turned around and saw the bundle of Shum's bones, intact and neatly knotted, ready to be returned to China.

# Historical Afterword

The description of the parade in this book is fictional. But the riot really happened. It started out as a parade, but soon turned violent.

On the evening of Saturday, September 7, 1907, Vancouver's *Asiatic Exclusion League* staged a parade to call for an end to Asian immigration into Canada. *The League* had two thousand members, including some three hundred professionals and merchants. Fraternal organizations, ex-servicemen and the city's fifty-eight trade unions all supported the event.

With a brass band playing patriotic airs, the parade travelled up to the old City Hall for a series of anti-Asian speeches. Eight or nine thousand men had gathered, but only two thousand could fit into the hall. From time to time, speakers came out of City Hall to address them.

The crowds drifted into Chinatown, just a block away. Shortly after 9:00 p.m., someone pitched a rock through a store window. The crowd erupted. Sticks, stones, bricks and bottles filled the air as the mob rampaged through Chinatown.

The destruction lasted only five minutes. Then the rioters headed toward Japantown.

The next day, crowds tried several times to invade Chinatown, but the area was roped off and guarded by police. The Chinese carried rocks, bottles and bricks to the tops of their buildings to hurl at the rioters if they tried to come through again. On Monday morning, the Chinese hurried to buy guns.

Then they held a general strike for three days. Hundreds of Chinese left their jobs. Downtown hotels and restaurants, West End homes, steamers, logging camps and shingle mills were all suddenly inconvenienced. Major Chinese landowners hired a small army of watchmen to guard their property against attacks.

In May of 1908, the federal government conducted hearings into the riot in Vancouver. The merchants of Chinatown were awarded over $3,000 for property damage (mostly broken windows) and over $20,000 for business losses suffered in the days after the riot.